# BECAUSE YOU
# DESPISE ME

## J.S. COOK

DSP PUBLICATIONS

Published by

## DSP PUBLICATIONS

5032 Capital Circle SW, Suite 2, PMB# 279, Tallahassee, FL 32305-7886  USA
www.dsppublications.com





ISBN: 978-1-63476-350-9
Digital ISBN: 978-1-63476-351-6
Library of Congress Control Number: 2015945885
Published January 2016
v. 2.0
First Edition published by ManLove Romance Press, 2009.

Printed in the United States of America
∞

This paper meets the requirements of
ANSI/NISO Z39.48-1992 (Permanence of Paper).

# BECAUSE YOU
# DESPISE ME

# CHAPTER ONE

HE WAITED five minutes, then ten, then fifteen. At eighteen minutes past, Frederik Abaroa crushed his most recent cigarette and downed the rest of his drink. It would take him two minutes to get upstairs and into the room, provided he didn't meet anyone along the way, but that was the trouble with a whorehouse: someone was always coming or going.

He took a quick survey of the room. The club was crowded tonight, and the band was making a fair hash of Glenn Miller's "A String of Pearls" while several ersatz couples clung to each other in various approximations of connubial bliss. The drummer—a large, pale man with the florid complexion of a ready drinker—was bashing his cymbals with a wholly unnecessary vigor. The room was hot and close and smelled of sweat and too much cheap perfume. He saw Jake Plenty talking to the bartender while Maurice fussed with a tray of drinks. Jake's back was to the room, but Abaroa wasn't stupid. He firmly believed Jake could see out of the back of his head.

Abaroa left his table and crossed the main floor of the club by the most circuitous route possible, passing the central cluster of tables and threading his way through the crush of dancing couples. The sounds of the baccarat game filtered through the casino's heavy double doors as Abaroa passed, and he felt his pockets reflexively. No, he had lost enough in Jake's Paradise already this week. It wouldn't do to compound one error with another.

The red-and-orange floor tiles seemed to throb and pulsate, and the potted palms slapped at him with spiny green fingers. He was sweating. The brothel was one huge, rococo landscape, and he but a tiny flyspeck in the midst of it—an insignificant thing most likely to be crushed by the juggernaut of unstoppable events, trampled underfoot and forgotten as if he had never existed.

He gained the stairs with half a minute to spare and stopped to look back at the room. No one noticed him, but no one ever did. The Basque might as well have been invisible. The couples were still dancing; the floor tiles still pulsed and throbbed; Jake Plenty was still talking to the bartender. No one in Maarif knew who Jake Plenty really was or where he'd come from. He was as much an enigma as the French *préfet de police*, Nicolas Renard. Rumor had it that Plenty and Renard had served alongside each other in the *Légion etrangère*—the French Foreign Legion—distinguishing themselves at Gallipoli, but rumor was Maarif's second-biggest export and not always to be believed. Rumor also had it that Plenty had killed a man in San Francisco, in some dispute over a woman, but Abaroa didn't believe it. He didn't believe it because Plenty didn't seem the type to kill someone over a woman—oh, Plenty could definitely kill somebody, but a woman would be the least part of the equation.

As Abaroa watched, Jake turned and gazed toward the staircase, a half-smoked cigarette dangling from his fingers—but his glance was a gesture only, a means to ease the posture, and Abaroa was confident Jake saw nothing. He continued up the stairs, moving slowly, like a man in a dream or someone wading through deep water. His instructions were explicit; he knew what he had to do, and a great deal had gone into tonight's plan. Many more lives besides his own were at stake.

"THERE WILL be a train coming through Maarif. It will stop long enough to put down a group of Boches, visiting on behalf of Vichy." She fished a crumpled photograph from the depths of the djellaba and slid it across the table.

He examined it, then tore it into little pieces and scattered them on the floor under his feet. The fragments would mix with the dirt and sawdust, and in an hour or two, the face of Feldwebel Horst Stussel would be indistinguishable from the rest of the garbage.

"He has two exit visas, signed by General Weygand. He is bringing them to one of the girls, a blonde named Yvette. She has convinced him she is in love with him, and they plan to leave Maarif together."

Jake's girls came from various backgrounds, but all of them were beautiful, and all of them had been carefully selected to cater to patrons' tastes. Jake didn't allow anything too violent or too dangerous in Paradise, but within those simple guidelines, a world of pleasures could be had.

Luisa was from Barcelona and had trained as a dominatrix with the great-great-great-granddaughter of the Marquis de Sade— or so people said. She was easily six feet tall and wore a man's suit and men's shoes and carried a riding crop under her arm like a lesser Prussian general. Her thick, shining black hair was caught up at the back of her head in a tight knot, and she wore leather bracelets on her wrists. It made Abaroa shiver—albeit deliciously—just to look at her. Her prices were rather more than Jake charged for his other girls, but then, the things Luisa did took skill and training. "It's not just brutality," Jake explained once, "it's an art. There are men in this world who will pay for that kind of art, and I intend to get it out of them."

Rolande had been with Jake since the beginning, when he had come to Morocco after the last war. She was extremely dark and extremely beautiful—a dancer who had trained at one time with the Ballets Russes in Moscow. Some said she had spent time in prison and Jake had gotten her out, and she worked for him out of gratitude, but Abaroa didn't believe it. There was an evil gleam in Rolande's eye and anger in her gestures, and he knew whatever it was that enraged her would come out some day, and violently. Still, she could do things with her mouth and her muscled thighs and dancer's buttocks that a great many men paid highly for. A single night with her was said to cost a king's ransom and was worth every penny.

Yvette was, as her name suggested, French, from the luscious wine country of Bordeaux—a redhead with a tiny waist and full, beautifully shaped breasts that strained against the thin cotton of her country blouse. She enjoyed costumes, and her specialty was a trick she did with ribbons. It was Yvette whom Abaroa had come to see.

Each girl in Jake's employ had a room of her own in which to entertain her clients. The rooms were decorated according to each girl's personal taste, as well as her specialty. Jake had taken the precaution of having all the rooms in Paradise soundproofed, a measure Abaroa was personally grateful for. He found Yvette's room and, without knocking, cracked the door.

Yvette was nude, on her knees before the German, who was reclining on the bed with his legs apart, his cock in her mouth, and innumerable colored ribbons streaming from his backside and his private parts. He was dark-haired and dark-eyed—hardly the Aryan ideal, but Abaroa supposed that beggars couldn't be choosers, and maybe Stussel's relatives were more highly placed than most. He seemed to be enjoying Yvette's attentions, bouncing his hips and pressing himself into her mouth. Perhaps, Abaroa reflected, he ought to let the poor bastard come, to have one last *sieg heil* before Abaroa sent him roughly into his own personal night, but there wasn't time.

He slid his right hand into his dinner jacket and brought out a straight razor. Yvette tossed her hair and her eyes met his, but only for a moment. Abaroa stepped silently into the room, closer to the German on the bed but not so close as to be discoverable. He slid one hand underneath the German's chin, yanked his head back, and drew the razor in one long, deep arc across the throat. The blood leaped up, darkly red, splattering the bedsheets, the walls, and Yvette.

She threw her hands up to shield her face from the spray and fell back on the floor. "Is he dead?" she whispered.

"Yes." Abaroa helped her up. "Where are his clothes?"

"There." She was trembling. Abaroa gave her his handkerchief. "On the chair. His jacket."

Abaroa delved into the pockets and pulled out a thick brown envelope stamped with German routing codes. He opened it and pulled out a sheaf of papers, and a great wave of relief went shimmering through him. "Good," he said. "Good." He crossed to where Yvette was and stroked her bloodied cheek.

She was weeping. "*Vive la France*," she whispered.

"Yes," Abaroa said. "*Vive la France*."

He slipped past her and out into the corridor, walking silently on the balls of his feet. To casual observers, it would appear he was looking for something. There were no casual observers. Abaroa tried a door at the far end of the hall and found it unlocked. He spoke some quiet words to whoever was inside and closed the door again. Then he was moving down the stairs, descending into the noise and bustle of the club, and from there again into the darkness of the desert night. A keen observer would have seen he was, by that time, empty-handed.

CAPTAIN NICOLAS Renard, *préfet de police* for the city of Maarif, was generally repulsed by the sight of blood. It was so entirely unnecessary, he thought, to make such a mess. Renard hadn't actually touched any of the blood but couldn't stop wiping his hands on his handkerchief. It would take forever to get the stains out of the rugs, he thought, and as for the pale pink paint on the walls, well…. Renard allowed himself a mental shrug, a luxury peculiar to the Gallic soul, and stowed his handkerchief in an inside pocket.

"I want everything he left behind," he said. "Go over this entire room with a toothcomb." He stood well away from his men, watching their progress closely but not interfering. Renard, unlike many others of his ilk, had absolute faith in his men to carry out their duties with efficiency and tact. He had trained them, after all. He had not expressly forbidden Jake's girls to gather in the doorway and watch the proceedings with horrified fascination, and besides, the presence of several scantily clad prostitutes—many of them hanging on his every gesture—could only enhance his reputation as a Frenchman.

Like most of his countrymen, Renard was vain of his figure and his dress. At forty-five, he was still trim and remarkably fit, and he kept himself that way by swimming in the sea every morning before breakfast. He was just under five and a half feet tall, more than sufficient for a Frenchman, and his body underneath his clothes was the lithe, taut-muscled body of a habitual swimmer. There was an expression of mocking good humor in his brown eyes, overlaid with a little sadness, and his ridiculously clean hands were gentle. He had been married once, or so the stories went, but it ended tragically. He kept no mistress as far as anyone in Maarif knew, and it was whispered that the only reason he visited Jake's Paradise was to see Jake.

"Nicolas, what the hell is going on here?" Jake Plenty shoved his way into the room. "You trying to close me down?"

"Ah, Jake, my boy, there you are." Renard cocked an eyebrow in his direction. "Do come in, but be careful where you are stepping. I'm afraid your murderer has left rather a large mess behind him." Renard spoke the King's English remarkably well and with an upper-class accent, the unavoidable result of his having been raised by his maiden Aunt Dimity in Dover from the age of seven.

"Murderer?" Jake looked terrible: pale and drawn, his face pouchy with exhaustion. Renard filed this information away, with all the other little bits of things he had noticed about Jake over the years. "What are you talking about?" He stopped short, his gaze irresistibly drawn to the blood.

It was the same with everyone, Renard reflected: once they'd seen the blood, it was all they saw. He took out his handkerchief, wiped his hands again.

"Someone has been murdered in this room. Judging by the volume of blood, I'd say it was a man and that he had his throat cut." Renard crouched and waved his hand over the stain. "You can see the way it happened. The throat was quite handily slit from ear to ear.

That's the only way to do it, if you're at all serious. The murderer was right-handed." He straightened, knee joints protesting, and positioned himself against the wall, just behind the bed. "The victim was lying down, most likely on his back, when it happened, which means the murderer stood behind him, roundabout where I am standing now. He would have bent over, lifted the man's chin up, and slit his throat that way." Renard tilted his head to one side, a gesture that meant he was thinking. "He died quickly, if that's any consolation. The first two heartbeats immediately after the cut would have pumped out massive amounts of blood." Renard indicated the arterial spray on the bed, the resultant spatter on the walls. "He's probably got it on his clothes too, and in his hair."

Jake cursed fluently, walked half a dozen short steps toward the door, turned, and came back again. "A customer. Someone came in here and killed one of my customers."

"Yes, I believe so." Renard gazed at him curiously. "You all right?"

"No, Nicolas, I'm not all right. If this gets out—"

"If this gets out," Renard said, "Paradise will have gained an unexpected cachet. You'll be turning them away from the doors." He clenched his fists and fought the urge to wipe his hands again. There was a slight commotion in the doorway; a policeman with a camera pushed his way past the girls and into the room. "Photograph all of it," Renard said. "What a pity the body isn't here."

"You…." Jake blinked, confused. "You mean you didn't…?"

"Oh, no, Jake." Renard smiled. "I didn't give any order to remove the body to the morgue. I've no idea where it is."

Jake stared at Renard for several long moments while the girls twittered in the doorway and Renard's men moved quietly about the room, combing every surface for forensic evidence. "You didn't. So he just got up and walked away? Is that it?"

"Oh, don't fuss at me," Renard replied, archly. "It isn't my fault the corpse has vanished. And by the way, I'll be interested in questioning you, Jake, my dear." He reached into his tunic and took out a leather-bound notebook. "As the proprietor of this… place… you'll probably end up being my star witness."

"You think I bumped off one of my own customers?" Jake said. His gut did a series of small flip-flops, even as his face retained its usual impassive demeanor. He wouldn't go to jail, and especially not here, not even for someone as decent as Renard. He wouldn't allow anyone to lock him up in anything resembling a walled room, not ever again.

"I never said so." Renard flipped his notebook open to a clean page. "Which one of your girls normally used this room?"

Jake thought for a moment. "That would be Yvette," he said.

"Ah," Renard replied, "that glorious redhead! Where might she be?" If the girl had been in the room when the murder took place, she would have seen everything, including the man who'd done it. Renard amended this mentally: the killer was most likely a man, but he wouldn't be surprised if one of Jake's girls had taken a knife to a customer. Some men had no idea how to behave in the company of a lady.

"I haven't seen her. She came upstairs with that German, the one they called Stussi, but that was hours ago," one of the girls in the doorway said—a little blonde with the flat, muscled belly of a dancer. She was wearing a pink negligee with a pattern of roses around the bodice and roses in her hair. Like the other girls, she went barefoot, and her nakedness was tantalizingly visible underneath the sheer nightdress. She had probably come to Maarif from elsewhere, hoping, like so many others, to book a passage to America and freedom—until her funds dried up, and she found herself stranded.

It could have been worse, Renard reflected. At least Jake treated his girls like human beings, paid them a fair wage, and saw to their medical needs. Some of the other brothels Renard had seen around Maarif still gave him nightmares, and his office was almost daily flooded with complaints about filthy dives and girls imprisoned in white slavery. The allegations almost always came from the outraged wives of foreign travelers, overrouged middle-aged women who insisted that *no, monsieur would never frequent a brothel*. Renard always nodded politely and offered them coffee, took their statements, and pretended their feigned outrage was justified. On good days it amused him; on bad days it made him feel tired—and a little old.

"Has anyone seen her?" he asked the girls. None of them had. "Then she isn't on the premises?" Renard asked. He spoke to his aide-de-camp, Lt. Andine. "Take three men and go downstairs. Search the premises for the girl. And station men at each exit. I want to know where she is." He gestured at Jake that they should step out into the corridor. "Let's leave my men to their work."

The group of women parted for Jake like a sea of nubile flesh. "All right," he said, "back to work." He turned to Renard. "Nicolas, perhaps we might discuss matters in my office?"

"Would this offer include a brandy?" Renard asked. It was late; he was tired and his feet hurt.

"It might."

"Then I accept."


JAKE'S OFFICE was up a flight of stairs from the main floor of the "nightclub," but situated on the opposite end of the building from the rooms his girls used to entertain customers. Jake never really closed, but around half past one or two o'clock every morning, he would turn the place over to his Dutch barman, Piet, and disappear upstairs.

Jake's private apartment was sumptuously furnished with the best accoutrements money could buy: opulent couches and fine Oriental carpets, original paintings of desert scenes, and even a water pipe, although Renard had never seen him use it. Most things he had managed to find in the local souk, but some things he had had shipped in—the huge brass elephants near the street-side window, Renard knew, had come from India, probably via the black market—and others he had picked up on his travels.

Most of the foreign nationals in Maarif could be considered refugees, but Jake, who had arrived here before the war, was more able than most to afford the creature comforts. His walls were hung with swaths of printed silk in red and flame orange, and his four-poster bed, although large, was not so huge as to dwarf the rest of the furniture. He kept a desk in here, and a liquor cabinet, and the only access to his wall safe was through Jake's private quarters. It wasn't that he didn't trust anyone—he'd said this to Renard late one evening while they sipped cognac together in the gathering darkness—it was that he didn't trust anyone.

"Here." Jake handed Renard a glass of brandy and threw himself into a chair. He reached to loosen his collar and tie. "You aren't honestly going to say you suspect me."

"No." Renard sighed and sipped his brandy. "No, Jake, that isn't what I am going to say at all." He regarded Jake with genuine concern. "When is the last time you slept, hmm? Been to bed at all in the past few days?" Jake's bed—as both image and metaphor—gave Renard a pleasant thrill, but he kept it to himself. Renard's imagination—at least as far as Jake was concerned—was a damnable thing: much too eager to provide him with tantalizing mental images of Jake alone in his bed and gloriously nude.

"I'm fine." Jake lit a cigarette and contemplated the chessboard on the coffee table. He reached out and moved a piece, reconsidered, and moved it back to where it was.

"You don't look fine. You look horrible, if you must know." Renard lit a cigarette of his own. "Been having nightmares?"

Jake moved another chess piece. "No." He looked up at Renard. "Do you think one of my customers killed that guy?"

"No," Renard sighed. "I'm afraid I don't think that at all."

"What do you think?"

"Jake, I'm going to tell you something that isn't exactly common knowledge, and I hope you will keep it to yourself. In fact, I am going to insist that you keep it to yourself, on pain of arrest and imprisonment." Renard smiled faintly. "You wouldn't like our cells. They aren't very sanitary, I'm afraid. I know how much you prize cleanliness." He gestured at the room with his cigarette. "Look at this place, for instance. Utterly spotless. Doesn't smell at all like a whorehouse."

"Go to hell," Jake said cheerfully. He forced himself not to shudder. He was getting better at it.

"What do you know about the Resistance leader, Salazar?"

Jake moved the chess piece again. He didn't look at Renard this time. "Never heard of him."

"And now I know you're lying." Renard took out his notebook again. "Everyone has heard of Salazar. He was imprisoned in Drancy, awaiting transfer to—well, it hardly matters—but he escaped. That alone was enough to put him on the map."

"Salazar," Jake said. "Spanish?"

"The name Salazar is his nom de guerre," Renard said. "His real name is Christophe Picard—" He regarded Jake through narrowed eyes. "Ah" was all he said. He waited.

Jake moved chess pieces on the board, smoked his cigarette till it was gone, and sipped his brandy. The clock on the desk ticked away the minutes. He stood up abruptly and walked to the window. "Sometimes I hate your guts," he said. He shoved his fists into his trouser pockets.

Renard got up and went to stand behind him. It was very late—or rather, very early. The streets were empty, the good citizens of Maarif driven to their homes by the ever-present curfew. He stood close enough to smell Jake's aftershave lotion, the very slight must of the day's accumulated sweat, and the deeper, warmer scent of his body. Renard swayed toward Jake's heat, wondering if he would ever have the courage to reach out, to touch, to take what he wanted. He waited, listening to the gentle susurration of Jake's breath in the darkness. "Salazar is coming here," he said. "Salazar is coming to Maarif."


THE MORNING rays of the hot desert sun bothered Nicolas Renard's eyes. Some years before, at Gallipoli, his battalion had taken shelter in the cellar of an abandoned house and was shelled with mustard gas. Immediately after the attack, Renard, like all the others, rubbed his eyes, unwittingly scrubbing the corrosive vesicatory deeper into his corneas and blinding himself for several long, frightening months. He finished out the war in a Scottish hospital, wearing dark goggles and wondering whether he would ever see properly again.

His vision had returned in time, but he had been overly sensitive to sunlight ever since and insisted on heavy Venetian blinds on his office windows.

Standing with his aide, Lt. Andine, he forced himself not to blink or squint unduly, and the effort cost him. He would have a roaring headache this afternoon, no doubt about it. He didn't know why Vichy was sending a deputation to Maarif—the city had no official German presence and was hardly likely to excite more than a momentary frisson of interest on anybody's radar. There was nothing in Maarif of logistic or strategic importance. The only reason Renard could think of for a German delegation to visit now was Feldwebel Horst Stussel's murder—not quite the "inspection tour" promised by the official communiqué, but Renard knew better than to believe anything coming out of Vichy. The unofficial word was that Stussel had been the nephew of a particularly highly placed party official, and his murder in this North African backwater was something of an embarrassment.

It had been four days precisely since Stussel's murder, and Frederik Abaroa seemed to have vanished off the face of the Earth. He hadn't been at Jake's Paradise since Stussel was killed, and his usual flat—a shabby suite of rooms above a fruit stand in the souk— was empty. The rich foreign women—who seemed to provide the whole of Abaroa's income—found themselves disconsolate and lonely, with no one to take them walking on the Corniche or to listen to their woes over an aquavit in Jake's Paradise at night. They drifted around the main square of Maarif in their fine silk dresses, wearing the last vestiges of their prewar jewelry, and mourned the absence of the dashing, big-eyed Basque with the captivating accent and the lovely manners.

The prostitute Yvette had also disappeared, and some said she had been killed as well, murdered behind Jake's Paradise and buried somewhere out there in the desert. She had left all her paltry belongings in the brothel, including her shoes and a few pieces of jewelry that had been gifts from grateful clients. It was even money, Renard thought, whether her body would turn up. Corpses tended not to last very long in Maarif, and even before Stussel's murder, bodies disappeared with astonishing regularity—

—but never from his custody.

The roar of the approaching engines filled the air, and Renard stiffened to attention, as did Andine. "Here they come," Renard murmured. "I can hardly wait for this."

"*Mon capitaine*, if you are unwell...."

"I'm fine," Renard snapped—and immediately regretted it. Andine was only trying to help, but perhaps he didn't particularly want to be helped. "I dislike these sorts of situations. I have absolutely no desire to be here."

Andine didn't look at him. "*Oui, mon capitaine.*"

The plane bounced a time or two on its way down, but taxied to the end of the runway without incident. Renard arranged his face in a suitably receptive expression. "No idea why they're here. They have no business...." But the door was opening, and Major Aleksander Danzig was descending, trailing a little cloud of sycophants. "Here they are."

Andine leaned close. "Shall I have them killed, sir?"

Renard suppressed a snigger, but only just. "Remind me to give you a raise," he said. "Major Danzig!" Renard's salute was just that and not the expected *sieg heil*, but if Danzig minded, he said nothing about it. He was a tall, thin man, hollow cheeked and faintly cadaverous, with the slender white hands of an artist or an aesthete, and a petulant, rosebud mouth that appeared to be eternally pursed under his neat moustache. Renard had met a priest in Toulon who'd had exactly that same sort of mouth; he'd been imprisoned for diddling little boys. "Welcome to Maarif."

"So good of you to welcome me, Renard." Danzig's expression said Renard's welcome was notably lacking in the sort of civilities one ought to roll out for a visiting dignitary, and he, personally, had decided to take offense. "This place is quite unremarkable... quite unremarkable. I had expected something more civilized." He snapped his fingers, and a young blond man rushed forward bearing Danzig's luggage under both his arms. "I suppose it will have to do." He nodded at Renard, and the party moved across the tarmac. "I was quite unhappy to hear about the murder of this young man. Quite unhappy indeed."

"Herr major was most unhappy," the blond man said. He had the lunatic blue eyes and fixed expression of a *Hitlerjugend* graduate. "Most unhappy."

Privately, Renard remarked that unhappiness was probably Danzig's normal emotional state. "Right this way. I have a car waiting." As soon as Renard had received notice of Danzig's visit, he had instructed Andine to haul out the finest car in the police fleet and to have it shined and ready. Renard was interested in making the major's visit go as smoothly and as swiftly as possible. The quicker Danzig was on the plane back home the better. Renard didn't enjoy keeping up a façade, but understood the necessity of pretending, especially in time of war. Luckily, he dissembled very well and could assume certain attributes at will.

"Feldwebel Stussel was one of our brightest young men," Danzig said. "A credit to the party, and to the Führer. We expected great things of him." He set off across the tarmac at a brisk pace that forced the shorter Renard to almost run to keep up with him.

"I am sorry," Renard replied; he wasn't. "My car is just over this way, major." It would be unseemly, he thought, to break into a run, but Danzig was doing his utmost to make Renard do just that.

"It is curious," Danzig said, "that your investigation seems to be progressing so very slowly in this matter. We had expected better things of you, Renard."

*Oh, go to hell*, Renard thought. His premonitions had been right: the heat was making him cranky. "A shame about the papers he was carrying. I expect the Third Reich will feel their loss most keenly." This last was a stab in the dark. Renard had no idea if Stussel had been carrying anything at all, but Maarif being Maarif and this being wartime, it was a safe bet he'd been up to something, especially considering the influence of his family. It was an old policeman's trick, but one Renard used a great deal because it worked. "Still," he said breezily, "I suppose such things can hardly be helped."

Danzig stopped and stared down at Renard. "What do you know about that?" he asked sharply. "Hmm? Who told you?"

His sudden anger had a hint of madness in it, and the desire to do violence. For a moment, Renard honestly feared Danzig might strike him, or worse. His heart thudded painfully in his chest. He forced himself calm, leaned back, and gazed up at Danzig with guileless brown eyes. "Well…," he said slowly, "…I fear he may have let it slip… the girls, you see." Renard chuckled. "You know women."

Danzig let loose with a string of oaths. "How unsurprising," he spat. "Everything in this place is contaminated! I should have known." He spied the waiting car and quickened his pace; Renard struggled to keep up with him. "Why are you not doing more to find the murderer, hmm? Here I find you in the midst of a veritable crime wave, and you are doing nothing about it."

Renard bit the inside of his cheek and fervently wished Danzig to the devil. "Oh, don't worry, major," he said airily. "I am confident I shall have the murderer in custody before the sun rises tomorrow." He held the car door for Danzig, his smile indicating this was an honor he couldn't possibly leave to an underling. "After you, major," he murmured.

"Well, you will be able to enjoy your victory over your morning strudel." Danzig peered into the car's interior and stepped back to allow the young blond man to sweep the seats carefully with a handkerchief. Only then did he fold his long arms and legs inside.

Renard was reminded of a praying mantis or some other similarly vile insect. "Hardly that," he said. He moved to sit and was hastily intercepted by the blond man, who climbed in and sat next to Danzig. "My modesty would never allow it. And anyway, I always take *petit pain* for breakfast." He fixed his gaze out the window of the car, willing the skyline of Maarif to appear on the horizon.

ABAROA WAITED till it was fully dark before venturing back to Paradise. He wasn't so stupid as to think he could slip by patrols unnoticed. If there was anything unusual going on in Maarif, someone would see it, and that same someone would, like as not, report it to the authorities. The whole place was buzzing with speculation about Stussel's murder, and thus it was vital that Abaroa allay suspicion. It would appear very suspicious indeed for him to stay away from Paradise. He was as much a fixture there as Renard.

Abaroa dressed himself in his most unremarkable clothing, gray trousers and a paler gray shirt, and parted his hair on the opposite side. He wore no jewelry or scent and switched his usual cigarettes for a packet of the local brand. He caught a taxi to Paradise and waited as a bus disgorged a group of English tourists, all slightly intoxicated, chattering loudly to one another, and oblivious to their surroundings. He waited till the doorman waved them through and slipped in behind them.

The band was playing "Deep in the Heart of Texas," and people were singing and clapping along. There seemed to be an eager crowd tonight, and already Jake's girls were circling the floor, looking for the evening's first customers.

Abaroa took a table near the door and ordered a champagne cocktail to try to quell his nerves. He hated burying bodies. It was bad enough to have to kill Stussel, though Abaroa had killed before. One corpse more or less in a time of war was hardly an issue. But a dead body was a hard thing to conceal, and a dead body wearing a German uniform even more so. Abaroa had borrowed a car, driven out into the desert, and buried Stussel's body in the sand. He bundled the clothing with oil-soaked rags, set the whole of it alight well beyond the city gates, and scattered the ashes in the sand. Abaroa fervently hoped the carrion birds would find Stussel's remains before any human did, but one could never be sure. That was the thing about Maarif: you never knew who might be here, or why they had come, or what they wanted. No one in Maarif was what he seemed; everyone had secrets, and some of them—like Abaroa's secret—required the most delicate handling.

"You sure do get around, don't you?" Jake Plenty, dapper in dinner jacket and dark trousers, appeared suddenly at Abaroa's table. He was smoking his usual cigarette, and there was an uncommon tightness around his eyes, but apart from that, he was as inscrutable as ever. "First you vanish into thin air, and then you show up here. What's the story?"

"Please." Abaroa beseeched Jake with large eyes. "Please let me sit here, at least for a little while. I have had a terrible shock."

"Heard about Stussel, did you?" Jake leaned against the wall and drew on his cigarette. "Everybody's laying bets on where the body went."

Abaroa blinked at him. "Stussel? I have no idea what you are talking about." His pulse boomed in his ears and his sweaty palms slipped on the glass when he tried to pick it up.

"Yeah, Stussel's the one we found dead upstairs, in Yvette's room. A sergeant, I think he was." Jake's keen gaze fixed Abaroa in a terrible light, examined him, dissected him. Jake knew, Abaroa was sure of it. Jake knew everything, and he would turn Abaroa over to the police, and it would all be for nothing, for nothing—

"How unfortunate," Abaroa said. He forced himself to meet Jake's gaze as if there were nothing wrong with him, nothing wrong at all. *Why don't you go and bother someone else?* He couldn't very well say that. It was Jake's own place, after all, and he was certainly entitled to hang around wherever he wished. Abaroa got the distinct feeling Jake merely tolerated him for some reason known only to him. Under different circumstances and in the cold light of day, Jake despised him, Abaroa was sure of it.

"I expect the police will want to have a word with you," Jake said. He took his time bringing the cigarette to his lips, and when he drew on it, the end glowed a fiery red. "Rumor mill says you're the one who filled him full of daylight. Captain Renard will be fairly chomping at the bit to talk to you."

"Yes," Abaroa said, "I expect he will."

"If you did it," Jake said, "you'll do the dance, you can bet on that." He grinned an awful grin. "Or maybe they shoot guys in Morocco. I'm never really sure."

"Yes, that's fine," Abaroa said tightly. "Now if you would just please—"

Renard appeared behind Jake's shoulder as if summoned. "There you are," he said to Jake, "as firmly ensconced in Paradise as ever."

"Hello, Nicolas. Thought you were entertaining our esteemed visitors." Perhaps it was merely Abaroa's imagination, but Jake seemed to relax in Renard's presence, spread out a little, and there was something in Renard's reaction to him that piqued Abaroa's curiosity.

"Yes, well—" Renard was interrupted by the sudden and noisy arrival of several large policemen. "Ah, right on time." He sighed and cast a glance at Abaroa. "You know, I really am very sorry. It isn't anything personal, but business is business."

Abaroa's blood froze in his veins. He cast about for an escape, but the doors and windows were blocked. Renard had been thinking ahead: there were policemen stationed simply everywhere. "Why?" he asked Renard. "For God's sake, why?"

They seized him by the wrists and dragged him out, screaming and fighting. He kicked at them, struggled like a wildcat, but it was no use. They were simply too many.

# CHAPTER TWO

"NICOLAS, I don't have time for this." Jake turned from his account book to glare at Nicolas Renard with something less than goodwill. His head was aching abominably, and it was still quite early in the evening. Three days since Abaroa's messy arrest, and the whole scene still left a bad taste in his mouth. He hated the Nazis as much as anyone, and as far as he was concerned, Stussel got what was coming to him, but the fact that Abaroa did it galled him. He'd have never thought the little Basque had it in him, and he resented that Abaroa had left the mess for him to clean up. It opened Jake to suspicion, and that made him nervous. The last thing he needed was the local authorities sniffing around. "The damned place is full of people. Couldn't this wait?"

They had come early, drawn like hunting hounds to the scene of the crime, pulled through Maarif's narrow streets by the scent of blood. Renard was right: Stussel's murder had gained Paradise an unexpected cachet, and people were lining the street to get a look at the room where the German had been murdered. The ones lucky enough to gain entrée were gathered in small groups, chattering excitedly over drinks, sometimes shouting to be heard over the band. Nobody was dancing.

"I don't see what you're so unhappy about," Renard replied. He took a look around the brothel. "Everybody's having such a good time. It certainly hasn't hurt your business."

Jake massaged his forehead with two fingers. "One of my girls is missing, Nicolas. I take that sort of thing seriously. Abaroa killed a guy upstairs, and now he's missing from police custody. Maybe people are thinking I had something to do with it."

Renard's gaze was sympathetic. "Nobody thinks that, Jake, my dear. Least of all me. And since I am the *préfet de police*, I would submit that you have nothing to worry about."

There was something… just for a moment, just there, something passing so quickly that for a long time afterward, Jake Plenty would wonder if he had imagined the sudden flare of emotion in Nicolas Renard's brown eyes. It looked like admiration mingled with affection… or at least something very, very fond. Seeing it made him feel as if he were suddenly presented with an option that until now had not occurred to him to consider. "Can't this wait?" he asked. "Whatever it is, I'm sure it'll keep."

"No, but you see, Jake, my dear, time is very much of the essence." Renard looked as cool and composed as ever, in a crisp white uniform glistening with gold braids and medals. His hair had been recently trimmed, and his narrow moustache was groomed to within an inch of its life. "Come along, now." Renard took his elbow and led him through the crowd and outside to a waiting car. Maybe he was being arrested. Maybe Renard had finally lost his mind.

Jake yanked open the car door and slid in. "The heat getting to you or something?"

Renard made a moue. "Don't be cruel." He sat next to Jake and lit a cigarette. "You know, Jake, you're much too tense. It wouldn't hurt you to calm down a little bit, enjoy yourself. You never know— you might discover things about your fellow man." It was a pointless speech to make, but Renard made it anyway. He had known Jake for a very long time, in the last war and in this one, and, consequently, they shared a certain understanding. But Renard didn't fool himself that it went much beyond good comradeship and an appreciation of each other's qualities. He very much doubted Jake had ever really been in love, or been loved in return—or if he had, it had ended badly.

"My only interest in my fellow man, Nicolas, is how much money he has and how much he is going to spend in my place. You know that." Jake grunted as the car jerked into motion and pulled away from the club. It felt like someone had gotten inside his skull with a jackhammer. Renard's driver seemed to be hitting every pothole he could find.

"What a masochist you are." Renard looked him up and down. "Got a headache, haven't you? You will drink that dreadful American rotgut." Jake was as closemouthed as anyone Renard had ever known; the only way to get anything out of him was to jolly him along, ply him with gentle barbs.

"It's not the whiskey." Jake's fingers clenched on his knees, then released. "I don't like scenes in my place, not like that scene the other night… with Abaroa."

Renard smirked. "I see. Someone chip a hole in that stone heart of yours?"

"No. It upsets people, and when they get upset, they go and spend their money somewhere else. Anyway, Abaroa was nobody. You know that." The big car turned left past the souk, heading out of town. Jake wondered where the hell Renard was taking him. There was nothing out here except desert and a few large houses, mostly owned by foreigners or members of the local government. It wasn't an area Jake frequented. He preferred to stick to the dives he knew, like his own.

"Mmm." A noncommittal noise from Renard. "Everybody is somebody, my dear Jake. Even Frederik Abaroa. We have a complete dossier on him, you know… just as we have one on you."

Jake ignored this last. He had a pretty good idea what Renard knew, and most of it had been gleaned from their time together in the Legion. The rest, Renard had picked up since Jake had come to Maarif. Renard probably knew him as well as anybody did—he had certainly known him longer than anybody else had. "Nicolas, do you think he killed that German?"

Renard smirked. "Do you?"

"You arrested him. And, no, I don't think he did it. He hasn't got the guts for it."

"My dear Jake, you'd be amazed the things a war brings out in people."

Jake turned slightly, so he was looking into Renard's face. "Yeah. I remember."

Renard's smile faded a little. "*Rien ne pèse tant qu'un secret.* Is that it?"

Jake shook his head. "Nope. I expected as much when they captured me. You're wrong this time, Nicolas. That isn't it at all." The car bounced over a series of deep potholes; Jake was thrown into Renard. He flailed wildly for a moment but righted himself. "That isn't it at all," he repeated.

"It… has broken lesser men than you," Renard said. His voice was very quiet, and all traces of his earlier mirth were gone. "You know that."

"If you ask me, you pony up too much for Vichy." Jake abruptly changed the subject. "You aren't cut out to be a puppet, Nicolas, and you know it." Renard was looking at him oddly; Jake didn't like it. "What?"

"I'm savoring the irony, Jake, my dear. I do so love it when people are forced to eat their words."

They drove for a time in silence, the big command car roaming quietly through the empty landscape. A huge gibbous moon had risen over the desert, hanging low in the sky like a bloated balloon. *Nothing here is wholesome,* Jake thought. *Nothing is clean or normal or decent. Everything in this goddamned place tastes of ashes and deceit.* He was surprised at the vehemence of his own thoughts, or perhaps Renard's conversation had flicked him on the raw. Nicolas had a habit of bringing up things that were better forgotten. It was as if he expected Jake to pour his heart out, or some such nonsense.

"Here we are." Renard's voice broke into his thoughts. "Arrived at last and none too soon." He patted the driver on the shoulder. "Thank you, Victor. You know what to do."

The house was large, cool inside, and well-appointed in the traditional Moroccan fashion. There were blue and white tiles on the floor, and the walls, pale and spare, disappeared into the upper reaches of the house, supported only by the early evening darkness. Everything was spotlessly clean.

"Who's your housekeeper?" Jake asked.

A silent boy appeared out of the shadows and took Renard's coat and hat.

"This is Ali," Renard said. He stroked the boy's cheek affectionately. "He's like a son to me. Care for a drink?"

"No, I don't want a drink, and I haven't got time for games. In case you didn't notice, Nicolas, I've got a whorehouse to run. Now tell me what the hell we're doing here."

"So impatient, Jake. Really, you need to slow down, calm yourself, breathe the night air." Renard drew him toward the foot of the stairs. "Come upstairs?"

Jake's pupils flared and his mouth flattened to a thin, hard line. "I see. So this is business." He shrugged out of his coat and tossed it over the back of a chair. "Fifty American to start, and I charge extra if you want anything special. Oh, and don't bother going easy on me. I'm a professional. I'm not gonna throw a joe if you decide you want me to take it up the ass." He had unfastened his cufflinks and had reached for the knot of his tie before Renard stopped him.

"Jake." Renard couldn't meet his eyes. "Please. I would never—"

"Yeah?" Jake laughed, a hollow, horrible noise. "That's what they all say. Of course, you know all this. You got a complete dossier on me." His gut clenched into a hard ball the size of a walnut. He was standing outside his body, watching somebody else argue with Nicolas Renard.

"You listen to me!" Renard's expression hardened. He grabbed Jake's arm and held on, his fingertips digging into the muscle. "If I wanted to invite you to my bed, I would at least be polite about it, and believe me, Jacob Plenty, you would be a better man for the experience. I'm well aware of the chip—or should I say, the plank—on your shoulder, but bear in mind that I didn't put it there." He tossed Jake's arm back at him. "Give me a little credit, if you please."

He was flushed and as angry as Jake had ever seen him, and Jake's display of pique shriveled a little. He had crossed a line, and he knew it, but he'd be damned if he'd apologize. Nicolas had no business dragging him out here without any explanation and expecting him to be grateful.

"What's upstairs?" Jake asked.

"The last thing you would ever expect." Renard went up and stopped on a landing. "What I'm about to show you is—" His mouth opened and closed on nothing. "Jake, I shall be shot if Major Danzig ever finds out about what is in that room up there." His fists clenched. "I cannot stress this enough."

Jake's scalp prickled. "Huh. What is it?"

"You might as well know." Renard threw the bedroom door open with a flourish. "I can't help it, Jake. I'm quite dramatic."

In the bed, propped up on several fluffy pillows, was Frederik Abaroa—bruised and beaten, but quite recognizable and very much alive.

# CHAPTER THREE

JAKE STARED for several long minutes, wondering if maybe Piet hadn't dropped something in the champagne earlier. "Explain this to me."

Abaroa's hands were bandaged, resting on a pillow, and one eye was swollen shut. He turned his head at the sound of Jake's voice. "You brought him," he said to Renard. "I'm glad."

"You see, Jake, your little jab about Vichy hurt me very badly." Renard smoothed the covers over Abaroa's shattered body. "They broke his fingers, you know… every one. I got there in time to stop them from beating him to death, but only just." He took a breath, and his expression hardened. This was the face Nicolas Renard wore when he interrogated prisoners. "I'm trusting you with a lot. I hope you realize that."

Jake shook his head, trying to clear it. "You're…?"

"Free French," Abaroa whispered. "He is, and I am. That's why Salazar came here in the first place. Nicolas is his contact."

"I'm not a coward, Jake, you know that." Renard sat on the side of Abaroa's bed. "But you understand, don't you? The magnitude of our trust?"

It was a lot to take in; he told Renard that much. "So you and him…?"

Renard's eyebrows wandered up into his hairline. "Jake, you wound me. You will persist in assuming the most dreadful things about me." He regarded Abaroa affectionately. "No, I'm afraid dear Frederik has often rebuffed my overtures. Claims to be saving himself…." He sighed in an exaggerated manner. "I'm going to leave you two alone." He glanced at Abaroa. "Five minutes is the most I can give you, my dear."

Abaroa nodded; it seemed to cost him a lot. "Fine." He waited till Renard had gone. "Everything he has said to you is true. I had orders to intercept the German, Stussel, and take the papers from him. You know how difficult it is to find an exit visa nowadays, and a visa signed by Weygand? People will pay everything they have. Everyone is desperate to get out of Maarif."

"Yeah," Jake said sourly. "There's a roaring trade." *Welcome to the fleshpots of North Africa*, he thought, *where money means nothing and human life isn't worth a tinker's damn.*

"You have heard of the great hero of the Resistance, Salazar? I was told to save the papers for Salazar. I'd had word he was coming here. But Captain Renard's and my plans were disrupted when Major Danzig showed up in Maarif." It seemed an effort for him to breathe without pain. "Captain Renard had to take me into custody, and we had to make it seem as if my arrest was genuine. They broke some of my ribs before Nicolas managed to stop them. It was necessary that the… charade be convincing." He smiled gently. "Have I reassured you, Mr. Plenty?"

Jake turned away and swore gently.

"Do you know how dangerous this is? This little game the two of you are playing? Maybe Salazar"—he spat the name out like a curse—"can get his own visas. You ever think of that? Maybe he should do his own dirty work." It was so typical of Christophe Picard, so bloody typical. Just thinking about it made Jake angry.

Abaroa shook his head. "Five minutes… I only have five minutes. We can argue later. Salazar is coming here, may already be here. You have to get him out of Maarif. It's absolutely necessary. Without Salazar, everything that we have worked for falls apart. You have the necessary papers. Get Salazar on the plane to Portugal, please. It is very important."

"Portugal." Jake had no idea what he was talking about. "Somebody kick you in the head?"

"The exit visas signed by General Weygand. I hid them in Paradise." Abaroa tried to smile. "I made a thorough job of it."

"So you did kill Stussel."

"Yes. Yes, Mr. Plenty, I killed him. It was the only way, and do you honestly believe he will be missed? What is one less Nazi in the world, especially to a man like you?"

Jake mulled this over for a minute. He didn't care for murder—or for murderers. "Did you have to do it in my place?" Abaroa was right, though: one less Nazi in the world could only be a good thing.

"Unfortunately, yes," Abaroa said. He was getting tired; his head sagged back onto his pillows, and his breath sounded raspy and wet, the way breath sounded in a damaged lung. If a rib were to puncture a vital lung sac—or maybe some fluid had formed around the heart—there were so many ways damage could be inflicted, so many horrible things that could be done to a man, to bend and warp him and ultimately to break him.

*The pain can stop anytime, effendi…. All I want from you is a number, just a number. See, I will bend low, and you can whisper it in my ear. How many?*

"When a man is…." His eyes fell shut for a moment, and Jake started forward, but the Basque was merely resting. "Mr. Plenty… believe me. Why would I allow the Germans to beat me to a pulp if my appeal was not entirely genuine?" He smiled faintly. "There are very few real martyrs in war. You know that."

"Why me?" Jake asked. "Why Paradise? What made you think you could trust me?"

"I chose you," Abaroa said quietly, "because you despise me."

"YOU DON'T seem very happy, Jake… and I've even given you a surprise." Renard shut the car door, tapped out two cigarettes, and lit them. He handed one to Jake. "You look positively gloomy."

"Are you on the level? I mean, all this stuff with you and Abaroa… is this real?" He couldn't reconcile it, couldn't align the two: the Abaroa who hung around Paradise, gazing at the girls with his great big hungry eyes, and the Abaroa lying in that bed in Renard's house, his hands and body shattered beyond belief.

"*Mon Dieu!*" Renard stared at him, outraged. "*Plus ça change, plus c'est la même chôse,* is that it?"

"I might say that's what it is… if I knew what the hell that meant."

"Oh, come on, Jake. Your French is as good as anybody's."

"I'm not stupid, Nicky. I know you've got your fingers in a lot more sticky holes than my place." Jake drew on his cigarette.

"I'm a *policeman.*" Renard sounded less patient than he looked. "I would venture that it behooves a man of my position to have his fingers in one or two sticky… places."

"So you just waltz me into your house and show me Frederik Abaroa, lying in bed and looking like hell, and you expect me to believe it. Is that it?"

Renard looked away, but not quickly enough to hide his expression of hurt. "Yes, Jake, it is." He drew on his cigarette. "And now that you know, you've something to hold over me. I hope you realize that."

"What are you talking about?"

Renard leaned forward, his hand on Jake's closest knee. "Abaroa and I are Free French. Surely even you realize that I'm essentially a traitor!" He huffed out a breath. "It's not bad enough as it is, with the…." His gaze trailed away. "With the other thing," he finished.

"Ah, but you've put it about Maarif that you were married. You're the grieving widower and all that. I don't see what the problem is."

"I *was* married!" Renard snapped. "I was married, Jake. Or don't you remember? You came to my house, you met her—after I got you out of that Turkish hell hole you were in. You wouldn't go home, you said—so I took you home to Katja." He stared at Jake for a long moment, made as if to say something else, but changed his mind.

"I'm sorry," Jake said.

"No," Renard replied, "you are not."

"I'm curious about something, Nicolas."

"Pray, enlighten me."

"Did you ever tell your wife?"

Renard swore in French.

Jake Plenty laughed. "Now there's the Renard I know. Anyway, what are you afraid of? You think I'm gonna turn you guys in?" Something in his expression closed down. "That was the only time, you know. Despite what you might think, I'm not in the habit of giving repeat performances." His voice was deliberately light, at odds with his expression. "And the court-martial turned me loose, remember? What was it? 'Confessions under duress.'"

"I never really know what you plan to do, Jake." Renard looked terrible: his face drawn taut with worry and fatigue. "In all the years we've known each other, I've never managed to learn more about you than the barefaced facts of your existence. I don't even know your real name."

"*LA MAIN de bois,*" he said, "that's what it's all about, isn't it?" He sized up Jake and offered him a cigarette. "You know, this place made Napoleon Bonaparte."

"Yeah, I wonder what it'll make of us." He accepted the smoke— and a light—and nodded his thanks. He was young, absurdly young, but there was steel in him, if Renard was any judge of character.

"Mmm, you mean you haven't heard?" Renard nodded at the stone building against which they were resting. "It's make you or break you, my lad."

"So if they break me, I don't get to see that wooden hand?" Jake's ready smile did things to Renard, things he thought he had all but forgotten. "'Cause I was kinda counting on that."

"I'm not really supposed to ask," Renard said, "but what made you join? I know every man has his reasons."

"Well…." Jake grinned. "Why are you here?"

"Oh, that's easy." Renard flicked ash off his cigarette. "Like every other man, I'm running away from my past."

"Oh, I see." Jake made a comical expression of mock surprise. "As bad as all that? So what did you do? Was the girl pregnant? Is that it?"

"Yes." Renard tilted his *képi* over his forehead, shielding his eyes from the strong rays of the Corsican sun. "You Americans are so very perceptive, and, you know, nothing shocks you. That's something I like about you people. No matter what the scandal, everything is quite all right." He reached out and wrapped his hand around Jake's arm. "No, don't go. I'm sorry. That outburst had nothing to do with you, I promise." He held his cigarette between them. "The girl—or should I say, the woman—was expecting a child, yes. Whether it was my child is debatable."

"Oh, I see. The town bike."

"No." Renard shook his head. "No, and far be it from me to malign the lady in that way." He grunted. "Lady. No, not even that." He grinned at Jake. "Perhaps someday I'll tell you, when we're old and gray, hmm?"

"Are we going to be old and gray together?"

"Absolutely. I see us living out our days in some quaint corner of Paris." Renard used Jake's shoulder to hoist himself to a standing position. "We'll sit by the Seine and fish all day and you can paint my portrait."

"I'm a piano player."

"All the better, then." Renard shouldered his rifle. "You can write songs about me. You coming?"

"Who was she anyway?" Jake fell in beside him. "The girl you left behind?"

Renard's gaze was resolutely fixed on the middle distance. "She was my aunt's friend… I grew up in Dover."

"Wondered why you spoke such good English."

"Mmm. And now I've told you."

"You ever going back?"

"To Dover?" Renard stopped and gazed into Jake's eyes. "No. No, I shall never go back to Dover."

"What happened to the girl?"

"She died giving birth to my son."

There was, suddenly, ice water in Jake Plenty's veins. "I'm sorry."

"Don't be." Renard turned on his heel and set off across the parade ground, walking fast with his head down, oblivious.


"TELL ME one thing," Jake said. "What did you have to do… what did you have to promise Danzig's goons to make them stop?"

Renard gazed at him, the abyss yawning in his eyes. "Let me have my secrets, Jake."

The car stopped in front of Paradise, and they both got out. Renard leaned forward to say something to the driver, and the big car moved off into the darkness. "Jake." Renard's hand fell on his elbow, more tightly than was comfortable. "I should like to have a word with you later… after everyone else has gone."

"Sure, Nicolas!" Jake grinned, but the smile didn't reach his eyes. "You know where to find me." He walked swiftly away, leaving Renard somewhere behind him. He plunged into the familiarity of the brothel as into a healing bath. The band was belting out "Do You Dig My Jive?" while Piet shuttled drinks across the bar. The excitement over Stussel's murder must have worn off: the patrons were unusually quiet, the bulk of them spending their evening in the casino while a few occupied the tables near the stage. Jake's girls drifted here and there, making friends with the customers, enticing men to buy them drinks or to come upstairs with them.

"Mr. Jake, you seem a little sad tonight." Gisele—a leggy, green-eyed brunette—leaned close to Jake as she passed. "Something on your mind?"

"I'm just fine." He wasn't. His guts were rolling with apprehension, and the cigarette he smoked left a foul taste in his mouth. Every time he closed his eyes, he saw Frederik Abaroa's ruined face and broken hands, and he felt a little sick. How had Abaroa stood it? Most torturers had a finely developed tenacity that earned results.

*It can stop anytime, effendi, you just say the word, we will make it happen for you, yes? Say the word. Mmm? Say it? No? What about now? How many? How many are coming, altogether?*

Jake suppressed a shudder and yanked his mind firmly back into the present. Renard had said he'd stepped in to stay them from killing Abaroa but had stopped just short of telling him what, exactly, he'd done. Renard was as much a cipher in his own way as Abaroa. God only knew what Renard had told the Nazis—or had promised Danzig—to make them lay off.

And Abaroa…. Jake suppressed a shudder. He'd taken all that Danzig's musclemen had given him… he'd taken it… and they cracked his ribs and broke his fingers and beat his face to a bloody pulp. Jake gazed down at his own hands, flexed his fingers experimentally…. It hurt him just to think about the things the Germans had done to Frederik Abaroa. It must have hurt like hell….

He shook it off and turned his attention to a pile of credit chits that needed looking over. He wouldn't think about Frederik Abaroa; he'd do this instead.

He'd do this. With luck, there wouldn't be any more surprises tonight.

A frisson at the door caught his attention. He laid his pencil down and turned around, wondering what the fuss was about.

Oh, God.

No, not God—Christophe Picard.

The Resistance leader Salazar had come to Paradise.

NICOLAS RENARD let himself into his house and closed the door quietly behind him. Now that he was out of the public eye, he could relax and allow his shoulders to slump and his posture to betray the consummate weariness that dogged him. He winced as he sank into a chair near the door and bent to pull off his boots.

"Monsieur, let me help you with that." Ali slid out of the shadows, a towel over his arm and carrying a basin of soapy water. He laid the items down and bent to pull off Renard's boots. "You work too hard, monsieur."

"Ah, yes, I fear you are right, but it has to be done, and better me than one of Major Danzig's bullyboys." He nodded at the basin and towel. "You've been looking after him, then?"

"Yes, monsieur." Ali laid Renard's boots near the door. "He is sleeping quietly."

Renard patted his cheek. "You're a good boy," he said, "a very good boy. Have I told you that today?"

Ali grinned. "I cannot remember, monsieur. In any case, it won't hurt to tell me again."

Renard chuckled, pulled himself up, and went upstairs. He peered around the door of Abaroa's room, but he was sleeping peacefully, lying on his back with his damaged hands resting on a pillow that Ali had laid across his stomach. The windows were open to the warm night breeze, and a pinch of incense was burning in a brass dish near his bed. Sleeping the sleep of the just, Renard supposed, but he couldn't find it in his heart to begrudge the man. Abaroa had risked much to further the cause; he only hoped Salazar—or Christophe Picard—appreciated it. It was funny how he'd already made up his mind to hate the man, seeing as how he'd never even met him.

Odd how Jake had reacted to the news, though.

Renard mused on this as he went into the bathroom to undress. Of all the rooms in his house, his bathroom was perhaps his favorite. He had overseen its construction himself, hiring only the very best artisans available in Maarif, and it was a work of art. The two huge wooden doors, inlaid with brass, opened inward to reveal a high, vaulted ceiling stretching up almost to infinity, punctuated by two large arched windows that overlooked the courtyard and offered a more-than-ample view of the starry night sky. The tub itself was round, carved out of a single, massive piece of marble, decorated with polished brass fitments and boasting a crimson silk curtain that could be pulled around it for privacy while showering or bathing. Renard loved his bathroom; under ordinary circumstances, it would have cost a king's ransom, but in his early days as *préfet,* Renard had come into possession of one or two pieces of information related to a certain government official. His remuneration—a reward for the exercising of his native discretion—allowed him to outfit his beautiful bathroom in a style that appealed to the hedonist in him.

Yes, it was very odd, the way Jake had reacted, almost as if there were something there between the two of them, something his sources hadn't uncovered. Mentioning Picard's name made Jake very uncomfortable. Why was that? Renard's sources had indicated that Plenty and Picard knew each other—or rather, had known each other, in the balmy, prewar days—but that was the extent of Renard's information. It was unlikely he would get anything out of Jake. The man guarded his secrets jealously and considered almost any line of questioning an assault on his privacy. What the bloody hell was there between Jake and Salazar? It had to be something huge, as well as something deeply personal. It had to be.

Renard stuck his hand under the hot spray and stopped. He was a very good policeman, and much of his success came from his inability to ignore the little tickling of an idea at the back of his brain, the sort of thing another might call intuition. He recalled Jake's reaction when he'd told him Salazar—Christophe Picard—was coming to Maarif. What was it Jake had said? *Sometimes I hate your guts.* There must be bad blood between Plenty and Picard, some very bad blood indeed. Jake's bitterness, his disgust, why, it bordered on....

The grief of a lover scorned?

Renard stripped naked and examined himself in the mirror. The bruises on his abdomen had faded to an interesting green color, but the marks on his buttocks and thighs were as fresh as if they had been made that morning. The sheltered cove where he swam each morning was deserted enough that no one else ever went there, so he didn't have to worry about being seen and having to make absurd explanations. The bruises themselves were dangerous, not merely as evidence, but because their presence indicated something about Renard that he would prefer was not common knowledge. The world was so much more dangerous these days, and anything at all could betray a man. It was better not to chance it.

He stepped into the shower and grunted as the hot water hit the sore places on his body. The pain brought with it a flood of sense memories, powerful and violent.

*Spread his legs apart. Goddammit, I said do it! Ich will, dass er die Konsequenzen begreift.* A fiery pain obliterated everything; when it was over, he felt like he had been kicked in the guts repeatedly.

*You should know better than to interfere. We were merely questioning him. What right do you have? He is nothing to you.*

He could still feel the grittiness of the cell floor against his cheek, could still smell Abaroa's blood, the stench of urine, the Germans' stale sweat.

*I might deal with you myself, you never know. Humiliation, though, is better, is it not?* And Danzig had been huge, simply huge. *This is how we do things where I come from. Du wirst es bereuen, dass du dich eingemischt hast, du wertloses Stück Scheiße!*

He soaped his hand and inserted his fingers into his anus, rubbing hard, gritting his teeth against the pain. It didn't help, and he was glad Abaroa was asleep and couldn't hear him. He was certain Danzig had done something to his insides, and perhaps he ought to go to a doctor, but it simply wasn't possible. There were plenty of foreign doctors in Maarif, but a visit to any one of them would involve explanations and paperwork—and far too many questions for a *préfet de police* who was essentially thought to be a puppet of Vichy.

He rubbed himself until he felt the warm stickiness of blood, and then he bent forward so the hot water could reach the ravaged places and wash Danzig's filth away. Renard soaped up, washed his hair, and rinsed off cold. He wrapped himself in a bathrobe as he stepped out of the shower. The house was silent.

"You should not have done it."

Renard didn't even blink. "You're supposed to be asleep, my boy."

"Do you know that your surname in French means *fox*?" Abaroa closed the commode and sat down on the lid. "This occurred to me." He jerked his chin at Renard. "There is no point in hiding it. What did Danzig do to you?"

A rush of blood padded Renard's face with heat. "Nothing," he hissed, "and you will serve me best if you do not breathe a word about anything that happened!"

Abaroa ignored the threat. "Don't you think Lieutenant Andine might notice that something isn't quite right?" He got up and followed Renard out of the bathroom and down the hall. "He is with you every day, and I would venture that he knows you as well as anyone." He paused. "You're bleeding."

Renard lifted his foot clear of the tiny pool that had formed beneath his heel. "What do you want?" he asked wearily. "If I hadn't intervened, they would have killed you."

Abaroa extended a bandaged hand. "You are injured. You must have it seen to. Please."

Renard shrugged him off. "Ali will tend to me in my room."

"And the mess?"

Renard glanced at the trail of blood he'd left behind him. "Ali will clean it up."

"Is Ali going to raise you from the dead once Danzig kills you?"

Renard, furious, turned on him. "What the devil do you care? Danzig thinks you're dead! He thinks I had you shot! You are no longer part of the equation, my boy." The fury drained away as suddenly as it had come, leaving him weak and shaken. "This is no longer any of your concern."

*Eventually*, he thought, *this damned war will be over and—*
*It still won't make any difference. I will still be alone.*

*Sacré nom de Dieu*, such self-pity! Really, it was sickening. "Go back to your room," he told Abaroa, "and I will ring for Ali." He chose to ignore Abaroa's knowing look. "Really, I will be fine. Once I've had a good night's sleep."

He spread a towel beneath him and sat on his bed, leaned forward, and laid his forehead in his hands. The bottom had been dragged out of the world, and nothing would ever be the same again. Whether Danzig knew—or suspected—Renard's true nature hardly mattered now. Danzig had him. From this point on, he was entirely Danzig's creature, or could be made to be through blackmail, through intimidation. If Danzig wished, he could have Renard transported to a concentration camp, made to wear one of those fetching pink triangles they gave out to prisoners like him. Renard drew his hands away from his face and looked at them: they were shaking. Yes, he'd need something tonight. He could hardly be blamed for wanting that.

He rang for Ali and lay back on his bed. The throbbing in his torn anus was nearly unbearable, and he wondered how much blood he had lost.

"Monsieur, I will clean you." God bless Ali. He never asked questions, never raised an eyebrow. "Turn over, monsieur. I will bring some salve."

Renard stripped off his bloodied bathrobe and lay on his stomach on the bed while Ali's talented hands went to work on him. The salve smelled of honey, myrrh, and amber; the scent rose into the still night air and mingled with the fragrant smoke from Renard's *oud* burner.

Ali, silent and attentive, massaged the healing cream deep into Renard's muscles. "Open, monsieur, if you please."

Renard hissed with pain, but only for a moment. The cream cooled his ravaged tissues, soothing him. "Ali, could you…?" He reached for the young man's hand. "In the chest under the stairs. Only a little tonight, I think. It helps me sleep."

"Of course, monsieur. I will prepare the pipe myself."

Renard dozed while he waited, his mind full of images of himself and Danzig's bully boys, seen as if from a great distance. Danzig hadn't even ripped Renard's uniform. He'd undressed Renard himself, and his touch had been light, almost delicate. If Renard didn't know better, he'd suspect Danzig was enjoying it, except for his contempt—violently felt every time Danzig hammered himself deep into Renard's body.

"Your pipe, monsieur." Ali sat beside him while Renard indulged, watching carefully while appearing not to watch at all.

The shadows cast by the lamp lengthened and wavered, resolved finally into a tableau of himself and Jake Plenty, walking together in the desert, their heads and shoulders wrapped in *keffiyeh*s, their eyes and mouths invisible. Renard could hear Jake Plenty's thoughts, and Jake could hear his, but it didn't matter what anyone said or did. They were walking to the end of the world, and they would go on walking forever.

He fell into sleep as into a deep well. Ali pulled the drapes and withdrew silently, taking away Renard's bloodstained clothing. He would burn them in the courtyard in the morning.


JAKE STEPPED behind the screen that separated his personal table from the brothel's lounge area. His heart was beating a mile a minute, and his palms were sweaty. Salazar—Christophe Picard—stood at the door, gazing around him as if he owned the place and could command everyone in it. Damn him! Why here, why now? Oh, he didn't care what Christophe thought. So he owned a whorehouse. Nowadays that was looked on as providing a valuable service, and anyway, it was none of Christophe's goddamn business. Who the hell did he think he was, waltzing in here like—

"They told me I might find you here."

The sound of his voice made Jake's hackles rise. He stepped out from behind the partition, and the bottom dropped out of his stomach. Christophe Picard had aged, and not well either: the sharp ends of his bones projected from his suit, which hung on his skinny frame like a sack. His dark green eyes were sunk in their sockets, and his face, bereft of its soft flesh, looked peaked and ugly, gray except for two faint pink spots high up on his cheekbones, burning with fever.

"Christophe! Oh, my God! What have they done to you?" He caught the man as he swayed and nearly fell. Behind the screen, Jake loosened Picard's tie and dabbed ice water on his temples. He flagged down one of the girls as she passed and sent her to get Piet.

"You wanted me, sir?" Piet was short, dark, and compact—and dreadfully efficient.

"Help me get him upstairs," Jake said, "by the shortest possible route, if you please."

"No, not here." Picard struggled against them. "It isn't safe." He rummaged in his pockets. "I have the address—if you can find me a taxicab at this hour of the night?"

"Sure." Jake sent Piet outside to find a cab. Supporting Christophe, he walked to the brothel's rear door and to the waiting cab.

"It's important that I talk to you," Picard said. His head lolled back against the seat. He looked terrible.

"That can wait till after you've had a rest," Jake said.

"No." Picard laid his hand on Jake's wrist. "I know I have no right to ask anything of you—"

"Yeah," Jake said, wincing, "you got that right."

"I suppose," Picard said, "you believe yourself blameless too?"

Jake sat back and lit a cigarette. "Go to hell."

There was silence between them for a long time.

"I meant to tell you that Ormond died a few months back."

"That's a shame," Jake said, "and I'm truly sorry. He was a wonderful dog—much more civilized than his owner, as I recall."

Picard turned his head to look at Jake, his cheek pressing into the back of the seat. "You really are determined to hate me, aren't you?" He sighed. "If you only knew what I've been through these past few months: running, hiding, looking for—"

"Save it," Jake cut in. "I know you, remember? I've heard your schtick before." His hands clenched into fists.

Picard blinked. "My… schtick?"

"Maybe you should just save your strength until we get there," Jake replied.

Paris in 1925 was flush with prosperity, sunshine, fine wine, and Americans. Like many of his countrymen, Jake Plenty had come to France because he liked the country and its lifestyle. Unlike his countrymen, however, he had been there before the war.

No one really knew why Jake had come to Paris in the first place, and as for Jake, it seemed an okay place to be. When Franz Ferdinand was killed, Jake had foresight enough to know what was coming. He joined the Foreign Legion on a three-year hitch, renewed it when the war dragged on, and by the time he was demobilized, he found himself free and unencumbered in the greatest city in the world. But he wasn't clever with his money, and before too long, he was penniless, wandering the streets with his cold hands in his empty pockets, foraging in rubbish bins for scraps of bread. He took to waiting with the fishermen by the Seine, hoping someone would take pity on him and offer him their day's catch. It never happened. Instead, they would shout things at him, filthy things that had rather more to do with Jake's pale-skinned, brown-eyed American beauty than anything else.

At first he hoped to find work playing piano in one of the many clubs around the city. Jake's wealthy psychiatrist father had paid for fifteen years of piano lessons, and Jake's skill at the keys was considerable. The only problem was most clubs already had all the piano players they needed. Thanks to the Armistice, a significant numbers of young, talented men found themselves in Paris after the war, and some of them actually had experience working in clubs, not to mention a finely honed repertoire of modern music. Most of Jake's experience involved piano recitals in white tie and tails, in the company of classical musicians in fine concert halls. He couldn't exactly oom-pahpah it up with the best of them.

One day, walking down the rue Pigalle, he heard music coming from some old building and went inside. As it turned out, the pianist was a former comrade, a veteran of the Foreign Legion, and a member of Jake's old platoon.

"Tell you what, Jake. If you wanna make money, you came to the right place. Madame Fragonard's always on the lookout for new guys, and I can tell you that you fit the bill exactly."

"What sort of bill?" Jake wanted to know—but it wasn't long before he understood.

Madame Fragonard's was a brothel, catering to the male sex only, and party to an exclusive clientele, all of whom had been handpicked and admitted on the strict condition that they behave themselves according to the house rules, which were posted at eye level in various places around the building. Most of her customers were lonely married men, men whose wives partied till all hours with bohemians and *bons vivants* and who ran around spending money. The customers were amenable to a clean, nice-looking American who spoke the language like a Frenchman and could give suck with the best of them.

Jake's first customer worked on one of the riverboats. He wore a greasy pair of trousers, a striped sweater, and a beret. He sat on the bed and undid his flies. "You," he said to Jake. "Come here and suck my cock."

Jake got down on his knees and took the man's cock into his mouth. The man was coming within three or four strokes, bouncing on the bed and shouting, "Mother, Mother, oh Mother, Mother!" He tipped Jake five francs and left, and then another man came in— tall and blond. He didn't speak, but stripped naked and lay on the bed on his stomach. After a few minutes, he began to masturbate, rubbing himself against the mattress while Jake watched. When he was finished, he got up and handed Jake a fifty-franc tip. Jake later learned he was the Baron von Stuck, the lone survivor of a long line of Frankfurt degenerates.

It went like that all night long, until closing time, when Madame Fragonard turned the remaining customers out into the street and closed the doors. She poured champagne for all her boys, congratulated them on a job well-done, and went upstairs with a Corsican named Luc.

"He makes believe she's his mother," one of the men said, "and sucks on her tits. She likes that."

Jake wondered if this was a theme, and did all Frenchmen dream the same Oedipal dream? He asked Nicolas Renard that question once, and Renard laughed and said not all Frenchmen dreamed of women—something Jake already knew.

It wasn't a nice way to make a living. When Christophe Picard arrived, Jake had been there for three years, and he was thoroughly tired of the lifestyle and ready to make whatever reasonable change might present itself. When Picard appeared, framed by Madame Fragonard's huge double doors, Jake knew his moment had arrived.

Picard wasn't an American, but he wasn't really French either. His mother had been Czech and his father a Bulgarian wine merchant with a weak heart. It was this heart condition that carried Picard's father off when Picard, an only child, was still a boy. A resourceful woman, Picard's mother remarried, as soon as opportunity would allow, a retired Prussian army officer living on his sizable pension and the proceeds from his ancestral lands. He adored her and called her "baby," and young Christophe was raised with the best of everything. He was used to getting what he wanted, when he wanted it. And so, when he saw Jake Plenty sitting by the window, sipping a glass of champagne, and reading *Le Figaro*, he was intrigued.

He introduced himself and sat, then asked if he could buy Jake another drink.

"It would be worth your while," Jake replied, "if you bought a bottle. We could sit together and enjoy it, don't you think?" It was something Madame Fragonard encouraged her boys to do, and the more bottles a customer bought, the better for everyone, since a portion of the proceeds often found its way back into a *putain's* pocket.

"I think a glass would be fine for now," Picard replied. He was good to look at, tall and slender and well-built, but not bulky. He didn't have the weightlifter's physique that was rapidly gaining favor among the athletic crowd. He looked like someone who walked a lot, albeit slowly, moving from here to there and back again with no great sense of haste. His light brown hair was neatly cut, and his green eyes looked out upon the world with a certain measure of amusement. He looked like someone for whom life was an endless series of pleasant experiences. He opened a gold cigarette case, offered Jake a cigarette, and lit it for him. "What sort of benefits might I receive, glass-per-glass? Speaking hypothetically, of course."

"Well, you know, monsieur, I was never real good at speaking hypothetical." Jake narrowed his eyes. Maybe all this fellow wanted was to waste his time. "But Madame prefers us to consume it by the bottle—if you know what I mean."

"Believe me, monsieur, your meaning is not lost on me." Picard held his gaze, smiling, and something deep inside Jake's belly shivered and turned over. "A bottle, then. Veuve Cliquot?"

They drank for hours, sitting under the great brass clock in the main room of Madame Fragonard's house, while men moved to and fro around them and spoke quietly or made assignations and went up the stairs, two by two. At the striking of each hour, Christophe Picard took out his billfold, laid Jake's fee upon the snowy white tablecloth, refilled their glasses, and went on talking. He did this three times a week, for six weeks, until one day Jake wondered if perhaps Monsieur Picard might like to take things further and did monsieur care to go upstairs?

"What's the rush?" Christophe held Jake's hand in his, caressing the palm with his thumb, his fascinated gaze drinking Jake in, devouring him, enjoying him. "Have you another appointment?"

"No, it's just that I worry you might not be getting your money's worth," Jake said. He jerked his head toward the ornate banisters of the great spiral staircase. "Madame believes in satisfying all her customers. I'd be remiss in my duties if I let you go away still wanting."

"Do you know what I want, Jacob?" Picard leaned close to him. "I would like to pleasure you."

"Of course, monsieur. That's why I'm here, after all."

Picard closed his eyes and shook his head briefly. "No, you don't understand, Jacob. I want to pleasure you."

Jake swallowed hard. "But—why would you—I mean, is this some kind of—"

Christophe silenced his protests with a kiss.

"Please. Come upstairs with me now, hmm?"

Jake's bedroom was located at the far end of the hallway, a large suite with a huge four-poster bed and two Georgian windows looking over the Rue Pigalle. The walls were plaster, painted a pale, buttery yellow, with gold carpets underfoot and a private shower, toilet, and bidet just off the main room.

"Madame is particular about cleanliness," Jake murmured. "She insists on it." He grunted softly as Christophe leaned in to kiss him, parting his lips with the tip of his tongue.

Christophe pulled Jake's shirt out of the waistband of his trousers and ran cool hands over Jake's bare torso. "Beautiful," he murmured. "Mon Dieu, so beautiful…. May I undress you?"

"Go ahead," Jake said. "I won't stop you. You're paying for it." He sounded far more confident than he felt—this was so far out of his usual purview that he might as well have been on another planet.

It had been a long, long time since anyone had touched his body with the intent of pleasuring him. Usually, given his job description, it was the other way around. Sometimes servicing a client caused him acute arousal, which he, like the other *putains*, took care of by masturbating. Madame Fragonard discouraged liaisons between *putains*, and any man found consorting with his fellows was immediately dismissed. Similarly, she was not in favor of men falling in love and leaving her employ, simply because too many of them ended up broken-hearted and destitute.

Christophe did not speak as they lay together naked on Jake's bed. His body was lean and pale, his chest and belly sprinkled with reddish-blond hairs shading to dark brown around his sex. He smiled at Jake occasionally, in the pauses between kisses, but mostly he was silent, and when Jake reached between his legs to fondle his erection, Christophe gently but firmly pushed Jake's hand away.

"This is for you," he said. "Lie back and let me pleasure you. This is all for you." Christophe took Jake's cock into his mouth and sucked him, varying the speed and pressure just enough to keep him on the edge. He held Jake's balls in his hand and licked them, took them gently into his mouth, and warmed them with his body's heat while Jake squirmed and panted and begged to come. "You're too impatient," Christophe whispered. "I can keep you this way for hours if you let me." He cupped Jake's buttocks in his hands, raised Jake to his mouth again, and sucked long and hard until the combination of pressure and moist heat tipped him over the edge.

The climax was intense—a series of deep, throbbing waves that thundered through Jake and left him shaken and spent. When he could see again, Jake reached out for Christophe and pulled him into his arms. "That wasn't necessary," he whispered thickly. "You didn't need to—dammit, that's my job."

"Pleasuring you gives me pleasure," Christophe announced. "Giving to others is how I justify… so many things."

If this utterance was a little too facile for Jake, he didn't say so, and when Christophe asked Jake to come and live with him a few months later, Jake was more than ready. Christophe had a job lined up for him: he could play piano in a little brasserie around the corner from Christophe's apartment. And during the day, while Christophe was at work, Jake was free to amuse himself.

It was the first and last time he ever allowed himself to fall in love.

Within six months, Christophe had transformed from an erudite and accommodating lover to an utter bitch. It turned out that Christophe had pretensions of his own and a very specific idea of the myriad ways in which Jake, simply by being himself, was cheating him out of a musical career.

Moreover, Christophe had begun taking drugs, mostly of the prescription variety, which he would purchase or otherwise acquire from various shady, underworld sources. There were ugly confrontations in their home: *You're taking dope… what the hell is the matter with you?*

*Of course I'm not taking dope! I couldn't possibly! I'm allergic.*

*But I saw you buying it. I saw you.* A woman from across the street had come to the door with a great many little pills in a small, silk bag and gave the bag to Christophe.

*You're a liar, Jake. You always were a liar. From the first moment I met you, I knew you envied me and would do anything at all to lower me to your own level. You're afraid of me, afraid of my abilities. You can't bear to think that my abilities might surpass your own.*

Shortly thereafter, Jake left Christophe, as well as Paris, and didn't bother looking back. In the intervening years, there was sporadic communication between them, usually in the form of letters that managed to catch up with Jake no matter where he was and involved Christophe telling Jake what, in his opinion, was wrong with him. These always took the form of bitter, vitriolic accusations, interspersed with the kind of manipulative, self-pitying language that was Christophe's personal specialty. Jake did his best to ignore Christophe, but no matter what he did, the seemingly unending diatribe continued. Finally, Jake got far enough away that Christophe couldn't find him, and, eventually, Christophe became a distant, bitter memory.

Until now.

# CHAPTER
# FOUR

"YOU'RE STILL here, Jake. You impress me." Renard appeared in Paradise the next night, carrying his hat in his hand. The *préfet* of police seemed to have aged a dozen years since Jake had seen him hours ago. He slumped onto a stool and cradled his head in his hands. The brothel was mostly dark, and although a few customers remained, most of them had gone upstairs.

"Why's that, Nicolas?" Jake unearthed a bottle of Veuve Clicquot from under the bar and poured for them both. He pushed a glass toward Renard. "You look like you could use it," he explained in response to Renard's look of surprise. "You said you wanted to talk to me."

"Yes." Renard rubbed his face with both hands. "Might we… convene in your apartment?"

Jake grinned. "Planning to take advantage of my virtue?"

"Oh, Jake, don't tease me." But Renard's smile this time was genuine. "May we bring the bottle?"

Jake seized it and his own glass and put out the last light. "We may."

Jake's apartment was up a flight of stairs from the main floor of the brothel. As such, it gave him excellent access to the premises and the added security of remaining on-site after hours. There wasn't much happening in Maarif at night, especially after curfew, but sometimes people got strange ideas. Of course, he could have hired someone to stand as night watchman, but Jake trusted very few people, and no one enough to leave in charge of Paradise.

He had decorated the place thoughtfully with draperies and rugs he'd found for next to nothing in the souk, and with desert plants that didn't need much watering. There were the usual sofas and chairs, a wardrobe for his clothes, and a chest of drawers—all very practical and masculine. His one concession to pleasure was the huge four-poster bed, dressed with silk sheets and furnished with as many soft down pillows as Jake could find.

"You're quite the hedonist, Jake." Renard unbuttoned his uniform jacket and slung it over a chair. "I always suspected it of you." He stopped Jake from turning on the light. "I'd rather the dark tonight. Indulge me?"

"If you like." Jake gestured at him. "Sit down, take a load off."

"Don't mind if I do." Renard sat on the floor and stretched his legs out in front of him. The creases in his trousers were sharp enough to slice flesh. "I'm exhausted, if you must know." He held up his glass, and Jake poured more champagne. "But at least… well, what's done is done."

"What are you going to do with him?" Jake pulled out a cigarette and, after a moment's hesitation, sat on the floor as well.

"Abaroa? As soon as he's well enough to travel, he's on the plane. Perhaps on the same plane as Christophe Picard."

"Huh." Jake grunted. "I don't much care about Picard. As far as I'm concerned, he can do as he likes. What will Major Danzig think of your little plan?"

"Major Danzig can…." And Renard described a difficult and possibly painful sexual act. "Twice, if he cares to." Jake made to light his cigarette, but Renard stayed him. "Care to try something a little more… interesting, Jake?"

"Like what?"

Renard unfolded a slip of waxed paper. "The effects are quite pleasant, not at all stimulating… I should know."

"Nicolas, hashish is hardly legal, even in Maarif."

"Oh, Jake, stop fussing. I'm the chief of police. What am I going to do, arrest myself?" Deftly, he made a hashish cigarette with a little tobacco and lit it. The pungent smoke drifted up between them as they passed the reefer back and forth. "Anyway," Renard said between puffs, "I prefer to think of it as supporting local industry."

"Tell me about Abaroa," Jake said. The hashish was making him feel relaxed and easy. He laid his head back on the couch behind him. "Where did he come from? Who was he before? What did he know? What did he think?"

"Frederik Abaroa…." Renard let the smoke out in a slow trickle. The faint glow of light from the street illuminated his eyes and his enormously dilated pupils. "He came here from Algiers, or so I was told. We never know ahead of time who's coming. None of us do."

Jake drew on the hashish cigarette and passed it back again. "Salazar led me to believe there are quite a few of the… of you people."

"That's right." Renard loosened his tie. It was warm in the room, and sweat glistened in the dark hairs at the base of his throat. "The way it was told to me, Abaroa was born in Roncesvalles, France, the youngest of far too many children. His mother died when he was quite young, and his father sold him to an Algerian silver merchant, an acquaintance of his, when he was eight years old. That's how he came to be in this part of the world." He passed the cigarette to Jake. "Jake, is this having any effect on you at all?"

"Mmmm." Jake tried to raise his head but couldn't. "Relaxing."

"Well, good." A warm breeze drifted through the opened windows, teasing Renard's dark hair. His face was lit on one side, while the other was in darkness, and in Jake's intoxicated state, he thought that was a perfect metaphor for Nicolas Renard. "When he was twelve, Abaroa ran away from his master and learned how to be a petty criminal on the streets of Algiers—picking pockets, stealing things from the souk, the usual. By the time he was fourteen, he had stolen enough to buy his passage to Paris. At fifteen he enrolled himself in school. When the war broke out, he tried to enlist in the usual way, but apparently there was some weakness of the lungs that prevented them from taking him. That's when he came to our notice."

"What has he been doing?" It was much to take in, and fatigue, combined with the effects of the drug, made Jake woozy and unsteady.

"Running drugs, mostly—oh, don't look at me like that! Sulfa and such to the frontline troops, mostly in North Africa. He acts as a courier, bringing things back and forth. You'd be amazed at how easily Frederik Abaroa can talk his way across the most impenetrable borders, Jake—he speaks eight languages, all of them fluently—and yet most of us know next to nothing about him. Are you falling asleep on me?" Renard's hand brushed Jake's cheek, lingering for a moment on Jake's mouth.

"Nicolas." The lassitude spreading through his body made it hard to talk, difficult to think. He wanted to lie down on the floor and sleep. He wanted Nicolas Renard to lie down beside him on the carpet. "I told him he was—"

Renard kissed him. Jake just had time to register the warm impress of Renard's mouth before he gave in to the caress, grunting gently. He grabbed Renard's shoulders and pulled him in, deepening the kiss, opening to the tentative pressure of Renard's tongue.

And then it was over. Renard stood and fetched his hat and coat. "Good night, Jake."

He was gone before Jake could utter a word of protest. He went to the window and watched Renard's trim, compact figure walking swiftly down the street, moving in and out of the scant pools of light that were scattered now and then by the darkness.


ABAROA WOKE to the warmth of the desert sun on his closed eyelids. He had been dreaming: he and Jake Plenty were in an office building, somewhere in America, and he was holding Jake at gunpoint while he searched for something. Jake was smoking a cigarette, glaring at Abaroa with his hands clasped behind his head, and maybe Abaroa had a gun, but he wasn't sure. The more he thought about it in his awakened state, the more it seemed Jake had somehow overpowered him and searched his pockets, wanting money.

"My dear boy! You're awake! How wonderful!" Nicolas Renard appeared, carrying a basin of hot water and a towel. "How are you feeling?"

"A little better," Abaroa conceded. He couldn't shake the feeling that this was all some absurd illusion and he would wake up in his old house in Algiers, lying under the eaves and listening to his master's enraged shouts: *Aren't you up yet, you useless piece of trash? Get up! Get up!* "My hands still hurt." He examined them wryly. "I suppose these will never be the same again."

"Well, you probably won't be playing piano at the Moulin Rouge any time soon, but let's not get ahead of ourselves." Renard laid the basin of water on the bedside table and rolled up his sleeves. He folded the sheet down from Abaroa's bare torso, his motions deft and impersonal. Abaroa's chest was blotted with dark bruises, each the size and shape of a Nazi boot. "Care for a wash?" Renard smiled. "Hot coffee, perhaps? Dancing girls?"

"All of the above." It was easier for Abaroa to talk, to smile, now that the swelling in his face had subsided somewhat. He was grateful—and frankly amazed—that the Nazis hadn't managed to break any of his teeth. "Have you heard from Salazar?"

"No. Jake took him somewhere the other night for safekeeping. I'm assuming he's to stay there until we can get him out of Maarif." Renard washed him gently, stroking the damaged skin with the lightest possible pressure. "I don't have to tell you that the sooner we can get him away from here, the better." The sponge touched one of Abaroa's broken ribs, and he hissed between his teeth. "Sorry," Renard whispered. "I'm so sorry."

"Does Danzig know I'm here?" Abaroa leaned forward against the pillow Renard laid on his lap, allowed Renard to wash his back.

"Not as far as I can tell. He's been in Paradise, and Andine tells me he visited the *palais de justice* yesterday morning—ostensibly looking for me—but I've been keeping away from him." Renard stroked soapy water across the relatively unblemished expanse of Abaroa's back. "Not going to be able to do that for much longer, I'm telling you. He's bound to get suspicious." He eased Abaroa back into position. "Salazar, I'm sorry to tell you, isn't helping. I've been trying to hurry him out of here, but for some reason he's been wont to linger in Maarif."

"Yes, well… it's like the Hotel of the Damned, this place. You can check in any time you like, but you can never leave."

Renard lifted each of Abaroa's arms in turn and washed them. "I was hoping Jake might persuade him to leave. He can be very persuasive when he wants to be."

*There is something going on there*, Abaroa thought. Renard's gaze slid away whenever Jake Plenty's name was mentioned—as if the mention of the man excited some painful association. "You were out quite late last night," Abaroa said. "Well past curfew."

"Oh," Renard replied, "you must be getting better. Your natural curiosity returns." He folded the bedclothes away from Abaroa's legs. The level rays of the rising sun broke through the slats in the window blinds, casting thin ribbons of light over the bed.

"You aren't yourself this morning, Nicolas." Abaroa's keen, dark eyes catalogued a plethora of details that a lesser man might miss: Renard's pallor, his obvious fatigue, the new lines around his mouth. He held himself almost painfully erect, as if he'd been starched into his clothes. "What aren't you telling me?"

"Have to ask you to lie down now, my old friend." Renard offered an apologetic smile. "If you want me to wash your naughty bits." He tilted his head to one side. "Or would you rather I let Ali do that for you?"

"Go to hell," Abaroa said cheerfully. "Isn't Ali more your type?"

"Ali isn't my type at all."

There—Abaroa's agile mind leaped to recognition—right there, that was it. "Ah," he murmured. "I see."

"Do you?" Renard moved the pillow across Abaroa's torso to cushion the necessary pressure as he lowered Abaroa to the bed.

Renard moved slowly and carefully, but by the time Abaroa's dark head rested flat against the bed, they were both tense and sweating.

"Tell me," Abaroa murmured as Renard went to work, "who is the object of your affections?"

"I haven't the faintest clue."

"You're a very poor liar, Nicolas."

"Frederik, my dear boy, don't you know you should never antagonize a man while he's holding your prick?" Renard's touch was clinical, impersonal, and Abaroa was deeply grateful. Another man, a man of less conscience, might have made this necessary act humiliating. Abaroa merely felt as if he were in hospital. "There you are." Renard eased Abaroa back up in the bed again and fluffed his pillows. "Are you hungry?"

"Yes," Abaroa replied. "And thirsty, and I need to piss—Nicolas, there's nothing the matter with my legs. I think I might walk to the lavatory on my own."

"Oh, dear me, becoming independent in our old age." Renard raised his voice for Ali, and the young man appeared and hurried to Abaroa's bedside. "Help Monsieur Abaroa to the toilet while I fetch his breakfast, would you?"

"Of course." Ali reached to place Abaroa's arm around his own shoulders, careful of the broken fingers. "There is a man downstairs waiting to see you."

"A man?"

"Yes, it's Monsieur Jake."

*It is amazing,* Abaroa thought, *simply amazing how he settles a mask of blankness over his features, like someone pulling down a window shade.* "Hmm. What the devil's brought him out at this hour?"


NICE, JAKE thought. Renard's digs were pretty nice, even for a minor police official on wartime pay. The house was cavernous. With high ceilings to allow for maximum circulation of air, the building would remain as cool as a root cellar on even the hottest of days. The furnishings were tasteful and had obviously been chosen with great care, but there was nothing frilly or swish about the place. The walls were plaster, the textured, dark gold color peculiar to this part of Morocco; the rugs were, as far as Jake could tell, handwoven and of excellent quality. Madame Fragonard, in Jake's far-off days in Paris, had rugs like that on the floors of her brothel, but Madame Fragonard had no such eye for taste and harmony. Renard's house proclaimed that the owner valued substance over show, and that he preferred quality over mere depthless style. It revealed much about Renard himself, as did the paintings on the walls and the fine silk cushions on the low couches and the bubbling fountain in the courtyard.

"Jake, my dear boy! What are you standing there for? Come in." Renard's crisp white shirt was turned up at the cuffs, and he wore no necktie. The casual attire suited him. Renard was actually very handsome, but this wasn't news to Jake. Renard had always been comely, affable, and urbane, possessed of excellent manners and the most delicate sense of touch.

*I know it hurts*… mon ami, *I know… just one more….* The open cuts on Jake Plenty's feet were filled with sand and rocks, but Renard had picked the dirt out. Sitting at the foot of his bed in a little cottage near Toulon, beside a smoking fire with the smell of wood and moss… and Renard's wife, what was her name again? A Russian girl, yes, Katja… she was little and pale, with huge dark eyes. She held Jake's hand and wiped his face with a cool cloth that smelled of lavender and bergamot. She'd wept for him because he was in pain, and he'd cried too and hated himself for weeping like a child in front of his old friend. *Don't be ridiculous*, Renard had said. *It's just you and me, Jacob. Just you and me and Katja, and Katja is as silent as the grave, aren't you, my dear?*

Yes, she had been silent; he remembered now. She never spoke, and it wasn't until much later that Jake understood, and what he learned about her shocked and horrified him. For a great many years afterward, he wondered if perhaps Renard had only married her because he felt sorry for her, sorry no other man would have her, as damaged as she was. He wondered, too, if Renard had married her to cover up, and if so, he wouldn't be the first man to take a wife as camouflage. Jake saw such men every week in Madame Fragonard's house.

*Please don't tell my wife I've been here.... She would be so unhappy if she knew it.* They wanted things their wives could never give them: the embrace of a man's arms, the kisses of a man's mouth, the thrill of the forbidden. Was that what Nicolas Renard wanted?

When the inevitable hashish headache had kept Jake awake, he'd lain in his lonely bed and thought about that kiss, wondering what it would be like to do the rest of it, to do all of it, and not just stop at a single kiss. What was Renard like in bed? What were his appetites? He had known Renard for years, but in all that time, their friendship had never occupied anything except the usual sphere.

"I came to see Abaroa," Jake replied. "I wanted to apologize."

"Hmm." Renard looked him over. "I rather think I like you when you're contrite. But I'm just on my way to the kitchen to fetch a tray for him. Had your own breakfast yet?"

"I'm not much of an eater in the mornings." He followed Renard into the cool, tiled kitchen and waited while Renard arranged Abaroa's breakfast. "I'll have some of this coffee, though."

"Pour me one too." Renard gestured at the cupboard where the dishes were. "Cream and sugar. Go easy on the sugar, if you please."

Jake smirked. "You watching your figure, Nicolas?"

Renard raised one impeccably groomed brow. "Should I be watching it?" He waved Jake up the stairs. "He's improved a great deal. Still in pain, but I think he's turned a corner."

"Nicolas." Jake stopped him just outside the bedroom door. "About last night."

"Oh dear." Renard's brown eyes were flecked with gold, each pupil encircled by a golden halo.

*Strange eyes*, Jake thought. *The eyes of a prophet or a madman.*

"Why do I get the feeling that you're about to break my heart?" He huffed out a breath and shifted the tray on his hip. "Go on, then. Get it over with."

He'd lain awake all night rehearsing it, arguing with himself, debating whether any such liaison was but a wartime frippery or a flagrant madness. *We've known each other for a long time. Sometimes friends… you and I have been buddies for a good many years… you know when you… I have been doing some thinking….*

Now that he was here, faced with the man, his most facile words seemed to stick in his throat. "When all this is over…." He raised his eyes slowly to gaze at Renard, and there was heat in his expression. "I wouldn't mind."

"Jake." Renard's smile was tentative but genuine. "I have often waded into deep water, only to discover with astonishing veracity that my boots leak."

It wasn't exactly a declaration of undying love.

"Oh, I see." Jake buried his disappointment in the rim of his coffee cup. "Pardon me."

Renard pushed the bedroom door open, the breakfast tray expertly balanced in the crook of his arm. "Now, then, Frederik, my boy, look who's come to see you."

Abaroa was sitting up in bed, washed and shaved and wearing clean pajamas. The bruises on his face had begun to heal, and his bandaged hands rested on a pillow on his lap. He seemed glad to see Jake. "He's been very good to me, has Captain Renard… but it's nice to see another friendly face." He indicated the breakfast tray. "Have you had your breakfast, Jake? Another cup of coffee, perhaps?"

"Quite the situation you've got here, Abaroa. Bed and breakfast, full-time dedicated staff. How'd you manage that?" Jake refilled his cup from the pot on Abaroa's tray.

"Oh, it's easy, Jake." Abaroa's broken fingers made handling the cutlery awkward, but he managed. "Just get yourself beaten up by Nazis."

*I deserve that*, Jake thought. *Yes, I do.* "I need to talk to you. I want some answers."

"Oh?" Abaroa looked up from his breakfast, a smear of butter on the end of his nose. "Is everything all right?" He frowned, his breakfast forgotten. "Salazar, he isn't—"

"Oh, he's hidden away nice and safe. Everything's fine. And you've got butter on your nose. Salazar is scheduled to leave Maarif as soon as Captain Renard and I finalize his travel plans." Jake sounded much more affable than he felt. It annoyed him to be put in the middle like this, made to fall in with someone else's plans and schemes simply because he was convenient.

"I see." Abaroa swiped at his nose with the sleeve of his pajamas. "And when will Salazar be leaving?"

Jake shook his head. "You're the only one who knows. Captain Renard and his boys have been over Paradise with a toothcomb. Stussel was killed in Yvette's room, and now he's gone and she's gone—"

"Excuse me," Nicolas Renard broke in. "It strikes me that this conversation is a trifle academic at this point."

"Of course." Jake shrugged. "You only had him arrested to keep him away from Danzig. Anybody with a brain can figure that out, and Danzig will."

"Yes, but my dear Jake, what you evidently fail to see is the limit of my powers." Renard wandered over to the window and peered out through the slats of the blinds. "Until Salazar is out of Maarif, nobody is safe. Oh, I can have my men pick anyone up and keep him in protective custody, but if Danzig decides to start sniffing around, you realize that things are liable to get very uncomfortable for all of us."

"What's Danzig doing here anyway?" Jake finished his second cup of coffee and lit a cigarette. "Stussel shows up, gets himself killed, then suddenly the Germans are swarming all over this place. I don't get it. Since when is Maarif such a big deal?"

Abaroa adroitly answered the question. "Since North Africa suddenly became so much more important in this war. Sometimes it is the little things, the very small things, that make such a huge difference in the end."

"You see, Jake, my boy, General Rommel is rather more nervous these days, on account of some… shall we say, inconvenient Allied incursions into the whole of North Africa." Renard chuckled. "You yourself know that wars are often fought on many fronts, and Danzig has his orders. He isn't a stupid man."

"He's figured out that you guys"—Jake gestured at Renard and Abaroa—"are maybe not the welcoming committee he expected?"

"No, I don't think he suspects anything." Abaroa clumsily buttered a piece of toast. "At least, he doesn't suspect Captain Renard. He has no information. He's hoping that if he stays here long enough, he'll find some. Perhaps along the way, he will find out who killed Stussel and be the hero of the piece."

"Well, you can bet he knows that Salazar is here." Jake shook his head. "You guys are crazy. I mean, really off your nut. Do you think you're gonna get away with this?"

"It doesn't matter." Renard turned from the window. "It doesn't matter if we do or not. What matters is that Salazar escapes."

Something dark and ugly flared to life inside Jake's chest. "And it doesn't matter to your pals if you and Abaroa end up dead, or worse? It doesn't matter that Yvette is missing, or maybe she's dead too."

"My dear Jake." Renard came to him and took his arm. "As much as I would love to discuss matters with you, and that at length, I'm afraid now is not the time."

"What did you do with it?" Jake appealed to Abaroa. "Whatever it was you killed him for, what did you do with it? Is it in my place? Did you hide it there? I don't want any trouble."

"There won't be any." Renard's fingers closed tightly on his arm, a policeman's grip. "There won't be any trouble. In a day or so, all this will be over, and you can forget about it. There's no need for us to involve you."

"Involve me?" Jake yanked away from Renard. "Nicolas, do you think I'm not already involved?"

Renard's features assumed a neutral expression. "I beg your pardon." He plucked an imaginary piece of lint off the front of his shirt. "Where is he?"

"Safe, for now." Jake was angry, and he didn't like the feeling. He didn't like losing control of his emotions—it was dangerous. "What was Stussel carrying? Why did you kill him? What did you do with it? And while we're at it, where's Yvette?"

THE HOTEL where Christophe Picard was staying wasn't exactly to his liking. It was on the far edge of Maarif, close enough to the desert that he could smell the dry heat of the sand, but near enough to the town's refuse dump that he could smell that as well. Perhaps that was Jake's way of punishing him, and if so, that was fine. Doubtless a man like Jake needed that sort of petty outlet for his feelings.

Picard's room was little more than a dark cell with a louvered door that didn't lock and one shuttered window looking over the refuse dump. All day long, Picard listened to the cries of vultures and other carrion birds while the hot sun baked the little room and sent the temperature soaring. To distract himself, he read books and wrote coded letters that would, with any luck at all, eventually find themselves into the vast and sprawling spy network of which he was a part.

If asked directly, Picard would modestly deny he was anything more than a mere cog in an enormous machine, a homunculus of flesh and human imagination. Secretly he fancied himself a modern-day apostle, sending letters to the faithful from his place of exile. It was enough to do even this little he was asked. It seemed fitting to give oneself, body and soul, to one's ideals. It had been a long time since he had given himself to anything—or anyone—else. He had never been in love until he met Jacob Plenty, but one look at the dark-haired young American, so confident—almost brash, in his American way— and Picard had fallen hard. Plenty told him the same sort of story they all had in those days: he had been in the war, been shelled at Gallipoli and eventually captured by the Turks. He'd spent time in a Turkish prison, in a cell little more than a hole in the ground, and by the time he finally escaped his captors, he'd been there for a year.

*How did you survive? How ever did you survive, my beautiful Jacob?*

*Oh, I'm not so tough. I think you'll find that if you need to, you can survive almost anything.*

It was true. Early in this war, Picard himself was captured by the Nazis and interned in Drancy. He entirely expected to be shipped to one of the death camps, Dachau or Belsen, and done away with. He anticipated such an outcome, and some part of him looked forward to it. He would die in the service of the cause. He had underestimated his own strong will to survive, and when some of the other prisoners planned an escape, he'd gone along with them, vaulting over the wall and escaping into Paris in the cold of early dawn. By then, he and Jacob Plenty had been twenty years apart, each entombed in his own separate sphere of personal bitterness.

He'd been surprised, to say the least, to find Jake had set himself up in business. He hadn't thought the American had it in him. Jake seemed to be the sort of man who expected things to come to him and, when his desires didn't immediately materialize, would become frustrated and bitter. *He isn't like me*, Picard thought. *At least I have patience.* He had become used to waiting, all during the long course of this war: waiting in this shelter or that, hidden by friends and allies, shuttled to and fro. It was necessary, and he was glad to do it, but he wasn't under any illusions about the outcome. He didn't expect ticker tape parades or a hero's welcome.

*Tell me: what do you want from your life?* Lying in blissful repose with Jake Plenty one hot summer afternoon, naked in their bed with the July sun pouring in the opened windows and the warm breezes drying the sweat of their exertions. *What sorts of dreams do you have, Jacob?*

*Oh, I ain't fussy. I just want good weather and good wine and to get laid as often as I can.*

A rap at the door jolted Picard from his reverie. He laid his pen down, got up, and moved cautiously toward the other side of the room. "Who is it?"

"It's me." Jake's voice. "Open up."

Jake stepped through, clutching a paper sack and a bottle of wine. "Here." He laid them on the table. "I brought you some food. You better eat up. I think it's better if we move you closer to Maarif, so you're ready to leave at a moment's notice." Jake didn't look at him any more than was strictly necessary and held himself apart, as if afraid a touch from Picard might somehow taint him.

"I just want to get out of here." Picard uncorked the wine and poured some into a cup.

"Yeah," Jake nodded, "that's what I want too."

"Tell me, has anyone called for me? Have there been any messages?"

Picard was trying to sound nonchalant, and failing. "You expecting some?" Jake lit a cigarette and peered at Picard through the smoke. "I thought you guys were supposed to stay out of the public eye."

Picard chose to ignore the jab. "I gave the police station as my address. There might be nothing." He shrugged, his thin shoulders rising and falling under his suit. "I am expecting someone to call and ask for me. I don't expect you to carry messages."

"Good," Jake said, "because I got a whorehouse to run, or maybe you didn't notice."

"Of course." Picard made as if to say something else but thought better of it.

While Picard ate and drank, Jake outlined his plan, sketching out the important points on a sheet of paper. "The best thing for you to do is to remember this and then destroy it. Danzig and his hounds might come sniffing around, but it's just vague enough that it shouldn't make any sense to them."

"There is just one thing." Picard offered the bottle to Jake, who declined it with a shake of his head. "Danzig isn't going to simply let me fly away from here, and the Portuguese are hardly likely to let me off the plane in Lisbon without the proper exit visa."

"Is that what Stussel had on him when Abaroa killed him?" Jake's gaze was hard and pitiless. "Because I wondered." He glanced around the room. "You need anything else?"

"Some explanations would be useful."

"I don't have time." Jake glanced at his watch. "I gotta go. I'll be in touch." He moved toward the door, but was stayed by Picard's hand on his shoulder.

"Do you hate me so much?"

Jake pushed the hand away. "I don't hate you." He sounded tired—*No*, Picard thought, *he sounds inestimably weary.* "I try not to think about you at all, in fact."

"I'm grateful… for everything you are doing for me." Picard offered his bravest smile. "Very grateful."

"Oh, I'm not doing it for you."

Picard blinked. "Who, then?"

Jake smiled, but it wasn't a nice smile. "That's none of your business, Christophe. In fact, it hasn't been your business for a long time now." He glanced around the room and nodded. "Keep your nose clean. I'd hate for you to end up dead before we get your sorry carcass out of Maarif."


THE TRUTH about Nicolas Renard was simpler than most people might have thought: he had become accustomed over the years to paying for what other people took for granted. Not sex—he had thus far never paid for sex, which seemed to fall naturally into his lap, in a manner of speaking—but other things. For instance, no one knew that once a week by appointment, a woman named Claire spent the night with him. Fewer still would have believed the reason why.

*Don't you think it's odd, my dear? I'm paying you for this.* Renard always gave her a fistful of francs as a token of his gratitude.

*People have paid me for far worse than this, monsieur.* That was the entirety of their business transaction. They would climb into bed together, and Claire would hold him in her arms. Sometimes they would talk about nothing in particular, and he would often fall asleep with his head resting on her generous bosom. He never said anything about the way he felt, and neither did she. If pressed, she would have confessed that being paid to hold *Monsieur le Préfet* in her arms made her feel quite sad indeed.

Renard whored himself—he insisted on being completely honest in the sanctity of his own mind—in other ways as well: he paid for the company of those he loosely called his friends, but not with money.

Ask anyone in Maarif, and they would have said Captain Renard was a man of influence, the person to whom you ought to speak if you had certain problems that needed fixing. His allegiances were generally believed to be firmly on the side of Vichy, an impression Renard himself took great pains to cultivate. In this way, Renard gathered to himself a loose circle of sycophants, ready to do *Monsieur le Préfet's* bidding, and a second, tighter circle of acquaintances who understood his personality and his proclivities and who were content to let him be—or even to encourage him in his vices, if there was something to be gained by that. A third circle existed outside of these other two, composed of former friends and protégées, most of whom resented him bitterly and would do him serious harm if the opportunity ever presented itself.

Today Renard had run up against a member of that third circle, and it was putting a serious dent in his mood. He had been carrying on a running argument with a subordinate in the form of increasingly inflammatory memos, and now that argument had come to a head. Renard had ordered a search of Jake Plenty's club and apartment, with the proviso that things be tumbled about but not actually damaged. His protégé had ordered the policemen under his control to tear the place apart, which they had gladly done. It was all for Danzig's benefit, and whether or not Renard's men understood was hardly the point. A murderer was loose in Maarif, Renard said, and it was important that they find him. He had killed a young officer of the Reich and had taken something valuable from his person. It was important to search the premises.

Renard blamed himself for not supervising things.

Naturally, Jake thought Renard had ordered the wholesale destruction of his brothel and was understandably upset. Renard had spent the greater part of the morning talking Jake down and prying the metaphorical knife from between his shoulder blades. Right now he was sitting at his desk, peeling a hard-boiled egg onto a sheet of paper. Like everything he did, the operation was neat and methodical. It hid the roiling turmoil in his mind, the image of Jake's angry face, and the sound of the accusations they had hurled at each other.

*I knew damned well you couldn't wait to send your thugs in after me! Did you mean them to tear my place apart, or was that extra?*

*You can't believe I'd do something like this to you. After everything we've been through together? I'm your friend.*

*You, Renard?* Jake's disgusted expression had cut him to the quick. *You're nobody's friend but your own. I don't even know you anymore.*

It hardly signified. This morning's Jake was quite different from the Jake he had kissed the other night, sitting on the floor together, avidly exploring each other's mouths. He'd known enough to pull back, just in time—it would be a damnable thing to let Jake Plenty see how much Renard wanted him, and not for any of the usual reasons. He'd been carrying a torch for Jake for years, ever since their time together in the Legion, and Jake knew it, but Renard wasn't stupid enough to let himself fall into an affair. He knew the sorts of things the Nazis did to men like him, the special sections in their death camps set aside for people like Renard, and the grueling work that would grind away his life. He wasn't strong enough; he would never make it. It seemed an unnecessary price to pay for one night of ecstatic coupling with Jake Plenty, or even a kiss or two. And yet the memory of that one kiss still made the bottom of his belly clench with raw desire. Just thinking about the heat of Jake's mouth under his own made him shudder with want.

*Oh, listen to yourself. You sound like an addled* lycée *girl.* He regarded the egg with revulsion and, turning, hurled it into the trash.

"You trying out for the shot put, Nicolas?"

"Jake."

He tossed Renard a set of car keys. "Get your glad rags on. We need to have a talk. And I'd prefer to do it away from Maarif." He indicated the open door with an abbreviated nod. "Head south, will you? Let's see what our friends the Algerians are up to."

THEY DROVE in silence for a while, Renard handling the wheel of the big car with ease, Jake dozing in the passenger seat. Renard was glad of the quiet. He hadn't been sleeping well lately, and the latest furor with certain members of his staff had turned his usually affable mood quite sour.

"So, who was it?" Jake's voice sounded gravelly from disuse. He turned his body slightly in the seat. "Which one of your thugs tossed my place?"

"Morriseau." Renard steered the car around a bump in the rudimentary road. The streets had begun to deteriorate as soon as they left Maarif, and eventually they would be driving on sand. "He did it to get back at me." Renard shook his head.

"Get back at you for what?" Jake asked.

"I've no idea," Renard replied. "Wasn't he the one from Marseille?" Jake asked. "You took him in when he first got here… the fat kid with light hair."

"Yes, well…." Renard grimaced. "It's as they say, Jake: no good deed goes unpunished."

"That was nice of him," Jake commented, "after everything you'd done for him."

"You mistake the world, my dear Jake, if you imagine there's anything like gratitude in it."

"You're starting to sound like me." Jake thought for a moment. "If you're such a cynic, why bother helping someone like Christophe Picard? Or Frederik Abaroa, for that matter?"

"You haven't been home in a while," Renard replied, smiling slightly, "so I'll forgive you that impertinent question, Jake. To a Frenchman who has seen his beloved France devastated—" He was silent. "—I can never forgive them for what they have done. Oh, it's merely cheap sentiment, but it's all the explanation I have."

Jake nodded. "Yeah." He gazed out the windscreen of the car. The desert came up on all sides of them now, dunes rolling upon dunes, an endless sea of sand.

"Would you mind telling me where we're going?" Renard asked.

"Oh, you'll see when you get there."

"I don't trust you, Jake. For all I know, you're taking me out into the desert to kill me."

"I wouldn't do that, Nicolas." Jake reached out, patted Renard's forearm, and held on. Renard had rolled up his sleeves in concession to the searing heat, and his skin felt warm under Jake's grasp, but not uncomfortably so. "I mean, I wouldn't do it to you."

"You can't know how that warms my heart," Renard replied. "You'd have done it to poor Frederik Abaroa, though, wouldn't you? Before you knew the truth. That's the trouble with you, Jake—you judge too easily."

"Yeah?" Jake's eyes narrowed. "And you don't know when to shut up. Stop the car."

"What?" Renard glanced around him: there was nothing but desert. "What, right here?"

"I said stop the goddamn car!"

Renard did as he was told. They sat for a moment, listening to the ticking as the engine cooled. "Now see here, Jake. You should know I don't take orders, especially from you." Jake was suddenly close to him, gazing at him intently.

"You don't know when to shut up, Nicolas."

*So this is it*, Renard thought. *I wonder how he means to do it.* "Perhaps I should have a priest."

"Do I have to make you shut up?" Jake murmured—and kissed him. He held Renard's face between his palms and kissed him thoroughly.

*This is a bad idea*, Renard thought, *and I shall regret it. This isn't safe, not safe at all.*

"Goddammit, Nicolas, don't you get it?" Jake nuzzled Renard's neck.

"I'm afraid you'll have to explain it to me, Jake." There was a prolonged period of silence as Jake "explained" to Renard with lips and tongue how things were going to be from now on. For his part, Nicolas Renard was just as eager, and he had a mouth just as talented as Jake Plenty's, and so things quickly went from tender to torrid.

"Stop," Jake murmured, pulling away. He was red-faced and sweating, and the front of his trousers was suspiciously taut. "Not like this."

"Sacré nom de Dieu!" Renard swore. "What is the matter with you?" His own cock was tight with blood and throbbed in time to the beat of his heart. He experienced an insane desire to rip his flies open and let himself out. The idea of a tryst in the desert heat was tantalizing. He would strip naked, lie in the sand, and pull Jake down on top of him, their bodies locked together, sweat-slick skins sliding on each other.

"Nicolas, the first time we…." Jake hesitated, uncertain how to phrase it.

"Oh?" Renard murmured something filthy in French. "Is that it?"

"I don't want it to be a quick fuck in an automobile."

*Oh, for Christ's sake*, Renard thought, irritated, *now he's going to do the honorable thing.* "Jake, don't you realize I'm easy? A quick fuck in an automobile is right up my alley."

"Oh, no, I'm going to treat you like a gentleman."

"Do stop," Renard begged. "I may lose my breakfast in a minute." He glanced around them. "So this is where you wanted to go? What place is this?"

"Come on." Jake went around to the back and took out a duffel bag and a blanket. "It's this way."

"Oh, I see," Renard replied. "You're going to kill me and roll my body in that blanket. How inventive. That's what I like about you Americans. You're always thinking ahead." His untended erection was making him cranky, and for a moment, he hated Jake just a little. Why was the American suddenly so circumspect? He had to know how much Renard wanted him—how much Renard had always wanted him.

They walked a short distance from the car, finally crested the top of a dune, and skidded gracelessly down the other side. "This is what I wanted to show you," Jake said.

"Oh, my." Renard took a long, slow breath. "I've heard of the sacred oases, you know, but most of them have left me completely underwhelmed." This was an oasis in every possible sense and could not have been more perfect: a shallow lake filled with water from the recent winter rains and sheltered from the blazing sun by a spontaneous scattering of date palms and low desert plants.

"Nice place for a swim, huh?"

"You have such good ideas, Jake." Renard didn't bother unbuttoning his shirt but pulled it off over his head. He toed off his boots, dropped his trousers with great aplomb, and stripped off his boxer shorts as if he were in the privacy of his own bedroom. He had nothing to be ashamed of.

The water was soothing after the long drive, and they spent a great many minutes reveling in the feel of it against their bare skin, splashing each other and engaging in the sort of boyish escapades Jake had nearly forgotten… and when these entertainments paled, they came together in the water, kissing hungrily as their hands slid over wet flesh, touching, gently squeezing. It was as if their initial explorations that night in Jake's apartment had opened a hidden door into an unexpected realm.

"I'm sure someone is looking for us," Renard murmured. He lay on his back at the edge of the pool, eyes closed, letting the water lap against his naked skin, Jake lying next to him in a similar state of repose.

"I told Piet where we were," Jake replied. "Just in case somebody came looking."

Renard tilted his head and glanced over at him. "Somebody like Major Danzig? Or somebody like Christophe Picard?"

"I don't want to talk about him."

"I don't suppose you do."

"Everybody in Maarif's got secrets." Jake turned on his side so he could see Renard's face. "You see, Nicolas, you're one of those people who seems to say a lot when in fact he's saying nothing."

Renard's face darkened. "Let me have my secrets, Jake."

Jake traced the bridge of his nose. "Will you tell me one of your secrets?" His mouth hovered over Renard's, their lips not quite touching. "Will you tell me, Nicolas? There used to be a time when you'd tell me almost anything."


"So, THIS wooden hand…."

"Oh God, not that again. Listen, you've got to get past that. You're in it now, my boy." Nicolas Renard grinned at him under the brim of his white *kepi*. "If you must know, I've never even seen it. Apparently, they let you look at it for a minute when you've graduated. That's all I know."

"I see," Jake Plenty said, "*Legio patria nostra*. Is that it?"

"Very good, Jake. What else have you learned?"

"Is your name really Nicolas Renard?"

"Yes. Is your name really Jacob Plenty?"

"Not quite." He lit a cigarette, grinning. "But it'll do. Smoke?"

"Happy to relieve you of your fine Virginia tobacco. By the way, where on earth are you getting it? I've yet to see you getting parcels from home."

"Oh, I've got my sources."

"Do you know, Jake, my boy, if this soldiering thing doesn't work out for you, you'll make an estimable living off the black market."

"WHEN I was seven, my mother died—it was no huge surprise. She had been unwell for some time. My father was ill-prepared for the rigors of raising a boy all on his own, and so he sent me to his sister in Dover." Renard smiled gently. "I'll never forget it, standing on the pier with my father and waiting to get aboard the steamer that would take me across the Channel. I cried as if my heart were breaking…, which I suppose it was. He was crying too. It was horribly hard on him."

His father had awakened Renard early, washed his face and combed his hair, and dressed him in his best suit of clothes. He tucked some money into Renard's pocket and gave him breakfast: *petit pain* with fresh butter and jam and milky tea served in the earthenware cups that had belonged to Renard's grandfather Guillaume, who had been a potter by trade. Father and son sat together at the kitchen table underneath the wide window that overlooked the garden. The last of *Mère*'s enormous sunflowers nodded their heads under the tender ministrations of a great many bees. The sun was just coming up, and it promised to be a hot day. Already a blue haze hung over the town, and the air was unnaturally still. Renard's father ate stolidly without looking up, and when he had finished his meal, he took his cup and plate and laid them in the big tin sink at the far side of the kitchen. The house was made of stone and very old. It had been in the Renard family for many generations, and rumor had it that Napoleon himself had slept there the night before he embarked on his Italian campaign of 1793.

It was a long journey from Toulon, moving north across country until finally they arrived at Calais. *Père* had arranged for their transport by train from Toulon to Calais. He had packed a lunch, and they would carry a bottle of tea with them for Nicolas and wine for *Père*. They walked down the gravel drive together, and at the end, Renard turned and looked back, taking a mental photograph of the house. He knew, even then, he would never see it again.

"I didn't get sick on the boat." Renard lifted one hand clear of the water and rubbed his face. "I was certain that I would. I remember my father's hands on my face…." His gaze had turned inward, seeing something Jake couldn't see. "His hands were callused, as hard as horn… he kissed my forehead and told me to be a good boy."

"Christ." Jake shook his head. "That's harsh."

There was an older American couple traveling on the boat, and the woman befriended Renard and bought him tea and cakes from the little onboard shop. She tried to communicate, but Renard spoke no English, and her accent was so atrocious that he could make nothing of her French. "She was so very kind…. I'll never forget her face. It was tanned very dark, seamed like an old boot, with bright blue eyes and a sort of downy fur around her chin and upper lip, like older ladies get." Renard fell silent for a moment. "She was so very kind to me, Jake. I suppose it's because of her that I've always been kindly disposed toward Americans."

Renard's Aunt Dimity was thirty-five, vivacious, well-liked, and very beautiful. She had a large circle of friends, bohemian types, and they would all gather at one another's houses now and then to eat and drink and discuss things like art, literature, and philosophy. "When I was eleven years old, my Aunt Dimity's friend Adèle decided that the time had come for me to be initiated into the mysteries, as it were." He stilled Jake's hand against his lips and kissed the palm. "She came into my bedroom, coaxed me to arousal, and… relieved me of my virginity."

Jake concentrated on breathing. "Jesus Christ."

"Quite. She relieved me of it every time she came to visit, until I left Aunt Dimity's house when I was fifteen." He paused, lost for a moment in thought. "But this is morose, and I've had enough of that lately. Consider it, Jake: we are lying in a beautiful oasis under the wide sky, delighting in each other's company. What could be better than that?"

"Did you ever… did you ever tell anybody?"

"Only you. Just now." Renard's smile was brittle. "There is one other I intend to tell, when the time is right."

Jake kissed him. "Come on. Let's get out of this water before I shrivel up completely."

They spread the blanket on the warm sand and ate figs and cheese and drank one of the three bottles of wine Jake had brought and played a game of cards while the sun's rays shortened and the shadows grew longer. Once the sun went down, it got cold, and they started a fire using dried palm fronds and scattered bits of desert debris. They drank the second bottle of wine.

"Morriseau… what amazes me the most is the depth of his vehemence toward me." Renard seized a stick and poked at the fire. "He wrote the most… vile things." He shook his head. "Listen to me. You'd think I was a schoolboy."

"No, I don't blame you." Jake lit a cigarette with a glowing splinter from the fire. "I expect people to knife me in the back, but I'm still surprised when they do."

"Is that what you think I'll do?" Renard lit a cigarette of his own. "Jake, what exactly is it we're doing? And why are we doing it now? We've known each other for a very long time, and in all these years, you've never made any sort of…." Renard's unoccupied hand described a complicated figure in space. "…overtures." He drew on his cigarette. "Why me? Why now? Are you trying to prove something to this Picard?"

"I'm not trying to prove anything to anybody, Nick." Jake drew on his cigarette and tossed it into the fire. "You know me well enough…."

"To know when there's something gnawing at you? Yes, in fact, I do." Renard reached out and held on to Jake's wrist. "Are you sure this isn't an attempt to… oh, I don't know… *à la recherche du temps perdu?*"

Jake laughed. "No, that's where you're wrong, Nicolas. I'm not trying to recapture my youth. I was working in a whorehouse, remember. Why would I want to remember something like that?"

"It couldn't have been all bad." Renard's expression was hidden by the darkness, his face distorted by the flickering fire. He might have been smiling, or he might have been weeping; Jake couldn't tell. "You did love this man, once."

Jake nodded. "Yeah, I loved him. Seeing him the other day, I wondered… I wondered what I ever saw in him. And you knew, even before he came here, how I felt about him… you knew what was between us. How?"

Renard scooted over so he was closer to Jake. He reached for Jake's hand and clasped it loosely. "I am the *préfet* of police. That brings with it certain… privileges where information is concerned."

"How much do you know… exactly?"

"I know that you lived with Christophe Picard for quite some time, and I assumed, given your domestic arrangements, that you and he were… that you loved him."

"So that night… when you said he was coming here…."

*Sometimes I hate your guts.*

"Yes." Renard stroked Jake's cheek. "I'm sorry. I wanted to… to find out for certain. It's odd, isn't it? All the years we've known each other, went through the war together, and there is still so much of you, Jake Plenty, that's an absolute cipher."

Jake squinted at him. "You're not exactly an open book yourself. You know, I went through training with you, not to mention the war, and I never knew you, ah, liked apples as well as oranges."

"Well, strictly speaking...." Renard smirked. "I lean more toward apples, but if a juicy orange presents herself, who am I to say no?"

Jake laughed in spite of himself. "That's what I like about you, Nicolas. You're a real diplomat." Jake poked at the fire with a stick. "Frederik Abaroa is nearly well enough to travel. I wanted to talk to you in private, without having to worry about who might be listening."

"And here I thought you brought me out here to tempt my virtue with cheese and fine wine." Renard was silent for a moment. "No, you're right, and I have been mulling that over myself. Of course, Major Danzig will have something to say about it."

"Major Danzig thinks he's dead. You said so yourself."

"Yes, Jake, Major Danzig thinks he's dead, so what will Major Danzig think if suddenly there's a flight leaving for one of the great cities of unoccupied Europe and I'm rather too interested in the goings on at the airport, hmm?" He leaned forward and grasped Jake's knee. "Don't underestimate Danzig, Jake. I warn you. He may be a lot of things, but stupid certainly isn't one of them. He'll have had me under his eye—and you as well—from the moment he arrived here. This is a very, very dangerous line we are treading, the two of us. It would be better for you, in fact, if you disavowed any knowledge of me."

"So what you're telling me is that Abaroa is stuck in Maarif."

"I'm telling you no such thing, and you can leave Frederik to me." Renard drew abstract figures in the sand with the stick. "I've been in contact with the network, made certain plans. Frederik Abaroa is getting on a plane to Portugal, and from there... well, eventually he'll end up back in the network, as we all do."

"I'd like to help." Jake picked at a blister on his thumb. "How is Thursday night for you?"

Renard looked up from the fire. "For what?"

"For Abaroa to go to Portugal."

"And here I thought you'd left all your esprit de corps behind." Renard grinned. "You're so devious, Jake, my boy. That's something

I adore about you. Surely you know that." He tilted his head back and gazed up at the sky. "When I was a boy in Toulon, I would hang out of my bedroom window every night and look at the stars. I could pick out all the constellations. I knew their names by heart. I would imagine myself becoming somehow detached from the earth and gliding gently out into the sky like a bird. Did you ever have dreams like that?"

Jake shook his head. "I used to dream about being a concert pianist, you know… play at Carnegie Hall or something like that. I practiced six hours a day, every day, for years." He flexed his slender hands, looking at them as if seeing them for the first time. "I was never really sure if it was the music I loved or just the idea of being up in front of all those people and having them clap for me." He shrugged. "After a while, it seemed like they were just different sides of the same thing."

Renard lay back in the sand, his hands clasped behind his head. "I used to dream of floating off into the universe on a river of moonlight. You, on a river of applause." He closed his eyes. "I should love to hear you play sometime."

Jake left his seat by the fire and lay beside Renard in the sand. His graceful hands were gentle as he turned Renard's face to his. "I would love to play for you." He leaned down and captured Renard's mouth, easing Renard's lips apart with the tip of his tongue. Renard groaned and clutched him as Jake's hand slid down to gently cup his balls, rubbing him through his uniform trousers. Jake opened his fly, eased his hand inside, and held Renard gently while his cock grew turgid, heavy with warm blood.

"Jake, you don't have to…." Renard's tongue slid out and wet his lips. "I don't expect you… I mean…."

"Were you under the impression that you were going to have all the fun, Nick?" Jake nuzzled Renard's neck, opening the buttons of his shirt as he went, licking and sucking his chest and each of his nipples in its turn.

Renard's hand in his hair stilled him. "No."

Jake raised his head. "What do you mean, no?"

"It isn't safe. Anyone could come along and catch us. Jake, I wouldn't want...." He imagined a group of Bedouins stumbling upon them in flagrante, or one of Danzig's leeches. It wouldn't do.

"Shh." Jake gazed down into Renard's eyes as they slowly ground their bodies together, pushing themselves closer to the edge, which reared up much too quickly. Jake cursed and grunted when he came, throbbing the hot spill of his seed into his shorts. He hung over Renard, panting harshly as the aftershocks rippled through him and died away.

Renard raised himself on his heels, pushed hard against Jake's belly, and cried some heated words in French, his back arched at an impossible angle, his whole body taut and shuddering. They lay beside each other in the sand, side by side.

"What did you do," Jake said after a moment, "to make them stop beating Abaroa?"

Renard sat up and made a show of looking at his watch. "Good God, look at the time. Were you planning to stay out here all night?" He dusted sand off his clothes and stood, fastening his buttons.

"Doesn't look like it." Jake glanced past him. It was dark, but not so dark that he couldn't make out the distinct beams of a car's headlights coming toward them. The machine had barely stopped when Lt. Andine was out and running toward them, stumbling awkwardly over the sand as he came.

"Captain Renard! Captain Renard! You must come at once. It's terrible, simply terrible!"

*No*, Renard thought, *not Abaroa. They haven't found Abaroa. They don't have that much imagination.* "What is it, Guillaume?" He tried to sound as calm as possible. "What's happened?"

"Murder, *mon capitaine*. You had best come as quickly as possible."

It was warm in the desert, but Nicolas Renard's hands were suddenly as cold as ice.

# CHAPTER
# FIVE

RENARD ARRIVED back in Maarif rather more swiftly than he'd gone. The entire préfecture was in an uproar, with the telephones ringing off their hooks, but Renard was more interested in the murder scene.

"Tell me no one has been allowed near." Renard shrugged into the spare uniform he kept in his office for such situations and ran a comb through his dark hair, shockingly disheveled by the desert wind and Jake Plenty's fingers. "Tell me, Guillaume, that no one has touched the corpse."

"Of course, *mon capitaine*." Andine poured Renard a cup of coffee and handed it to him.

"This is monstrous," Renard spat, "absolutely monstrous! There was no need, no need at all." Privately, he wondered whether Danzig was behind this. Perhaps the Nazi intended to send Renard a message—it had that lurid flavor to it. Renard went to the front office and strapped on his belt and checked that his revolver was sitting in its holster and was loaded.

"But if *mon capitaine* will forgive me, there has been some talk of a speculative nature."

"What?" Renard glared at him. "About what?"

Andine backed away, hands raised in an inimitable Gallic gesture. "I am not the one who started the talk, *Monsieur le Préfet*, but there has been some… discussion about you and Monsieur Jake."

Renard advanced on him, dark eyes snapping. "What about Monsieur Jake?"

"There is talk that Monsieur Jake is your particular friend, and that you are his. I mention this because it might cause difficulty if Major Danzig were to hear of it." Andine raised his shoulders and let them drop, an expression of *le mal du siècle*.

"You have time to stand around listening to talk when people are being murdered, Andine?"

"*Mais non*, monsieur, but—"

Renard pushed past him. "Come on. We haven't got all night."

YVETTE'S BODY lay tumbled against the side of a vendor's stall in the now-deserted souk. She was naked from the waist down, and her body had been drenched with water, possibly to wash away the blood. On that score, the murderer hadn't done a very good job: the neck of her white blouse was red, and more of the blood had pooled beneath her head, probably from the enormous gash in her throat. It was horribly reminiscent of the way Stussel had been killed.

"He's nearly taken her head off," Renard murmured. He leaned over the body, not touching her, taking careful note of everything he saw. Her face was a mass of bruises, but that had been done at or near the time of death, judging by the color of the wounds. Her feet were bare. "Did you find her shoes?"

"*Non*, monsieur." Andine held the torch a little closer to the body.

"Barefoot." Renard wasn't talking to anyone in particular, but Andine was listening. "Judging by the state of her feet, she didn't walk all the way out here." He sighed and sat back on his haunches. "She hasn't been seen for days, and then she turns up with her throat cut. Someone's left her here for us to find."

There was a murmur, and the crowd around the scene parted to let Jake Plenty step through. "Nicolas? What's going on?"

"Mr. Plenty, I'm not sure you should even be here." The compassionate friend was gone; in his place was a steely eyed chief of police. "The girl was one of your employees, and you haven't yet been ruled out as a suspect." He stood back to let two stretcher bearers take Yvette's body away.

Jake ignored him. "Any idea who did this?"

"Not yet." Renard looked him over. "Have you got an alibi, Jake?"

"You're a funny guy, Nicolas. A real funny guy." Jake lit a cigarette and drew on it savagely. "You think I had something to do with this?"

"I never theorize in advance of the facts." Renard was grim. "You know that. Come, I'll walk you to your car."

"So it's murder."

"Yes, Jake… it's murder." Renard seemed to sag for a moment. "I guess it's another late night for me."

"Wait a minute." Jake caught hold of his arm. "Everybody knew Yvette. Who'd want her dead? She was no threat to anybody… she knew me, she knew you…."

"And she was servicing Stussel when he was murdered." Renard held Jake's eyes for a long moment. "That, perhaps, is incidental, but maybe not. There is also the fact that she worked for you."

"So it's me they want."

"Perhaps." Renard looked like a man in hell. Behind him, Andine was shouting for the locals to disperse and dispatching officers to push back the crowd of curious onlookers who had gathered around the scene.

"Well, what am I supposed to do?"

Renard held the car door open for him. "Go back to Paradise."

Jake bent close to him. "You think Danzig's goons had something to do with this?"

"I reserve my opinion until the proceedings of the postmortem." Which could take a long time, depending on when a reasonable pathologist was available to do the procedure. In Maarif, everything seemed to take three times longer than it did anywhere else.

"Give you a ride back to town?" Jake asked.

Renard glanced at Andine. "I'd better not," he said quietly, "but if you come by headquarters this evening, I won't throw you out."

"Something you're not telling me, Nicolas?"

"Later," Renard said. "Come see me later." He tapped the car door. "Good night, Jake."


JAKE WAITED a decent interval before leaving Paradise and driving over to police headquarters. It was well past midnight, and Piet was more than capable of closing up for him. The klieg lights had already begun sweeping the perimeter when he stepped into Renard's office. The place was quiet, with Lt. Andine and most of the other officers still busy combing the murder scene, and, since Vichy kept Renard horribly understaffed, there was no adjutant to show Jake in.

Renard was sitting at his desk filling out some reports. His loosened tie was his only concession to comfort, but the windows were open, allowing the night breeze to enter. He glanced up as Jake appeared, then went back to writing. "Have a seat, Jake. There's cognac on the table over there. Help yourself."

Jake poured two fingers of cognac into a glass and passed it to Renard, then poured another for himself. He sat in the chair next to Renard's desk. "I don't understand why someone would want to kill Yvette." The girl's murder had upset him: Jake, unlike a lot of other men in his line of work, cared about his girls.

"Really?" Renard's pen scratched noisily on the paper. "This is Maarif, Jake. I'm surprised more people haven't been killed, given the current conditions."

He was Captain Renard again, Jake realized. The playful and complaisant Nicolas of this afternoon had gone back into hiding. "Yet you serve Vichy, Nicolas."

Renard raised his eyes. "We are in unoccupied France, Jake. Even someone like you can understand that." He dropped some papers into the filing cabinet next to his desk, sighed, and took a drink. "And that was Yvette."

"Come on." Jake stood. "Let's get out of here."

"I really should…."

"…turn command over to someone else and go home, Nicolas." Jake hovered on the cusp of a decision, then plunged in with a mental shrug. "Or come home with me."

The message was unmistakable, as was the fire in his eyes. Renard felt a jolt of ragged lust go sizzling through him. "People will talk."

"About what? That you and I are seen together? For God's sake, Nicolas, they can come to Paradise and see that any night of the week."

Renard rubbed his face with both hands. "Andine is more than capable of bringing in a suspect, but between you and me, I very much doubt that Yvette's murderer is loitering round the desert waiting for us to arrest him. All right. Just let me get my hat."

PARADISE HAD long since closed, and Jake's apartment was cool and dark and quiet. Jake shut the door behind them both and turned the key in the lock. He made no move to turn on a light. "You're locked in, Nicolas. You've got no choice but to stay here now."

"I don't know if this is wise," Renard said. "Abaroa is…."

"…being very careful." Jake laid his hands on Renard's shoulders. "If there's anything strange going on, you'll know about it. As a matter of fact, so will I."

"Ah, yes." Renard unbuttoned his uniform coat, slipped out of it, and tossed it across the back of the sofa. "Your dubious connections." Jake took a step toward him and enveloped Renard in his arms. He was trembling.

"Good God, Nicolas… are you nervous?"

Renard laughed shakily. "Poke fun at me if you must, dear boy, but I'm a lot older than you, and this afternoon's frolic doesn't really count." He made a coquettish face. "Of course, I'm nervous."

"You know what I keep thinking?" Jake took Renard's hands in his.

"Do enlighten me."

"Nicolas, why the hell didn't we do this years ago?" Jake claimed Renard's mouth with a passion that bordered on violence, driving Renard back against the wall and holding him there, grinding his hips against Renard in a slow, tantalizing rhythm.

Some years before, Renard had been privileged to make the acquaintance of an American taxi dancer named George, an agile and athletic provocateur with the bearing and carriage of a Greek god and a talent for the oral arts that made all of Renard's intimate encounters pale by comparison—until now. Pressed up against the wall with Jake Plenty plundering his mouth, he felt wave after wave of sensual pleasure building to an unbearable tension, flooding all his nerves with exquisite sensation. And somehow, in the midst of it, without breaking contact or their kiss, Jake was busily stripping him naked.

Jake stepped away long enough to drop his trousers and pull his shirt over his head. His nude body glowed pale in the darkness, and Renard's mouth went dry with desire. "Oh, you beautiful thing." It was hard to breathe. "*Je n'ai jamais vu n'importe quoi aussi beau que toi*, Jake, *mon chéri, mon aimé.*"

He lay on his back in Jake's bed, his body thrumming with anticipation. He felt almost as he had on his wedding night with silent Katja all those years ago, moving to couple with her in the darkness of their marriage bed, parting her thighs and pressing his mouth to her body, tasting her, opening her, coaxing her gently toward the center of desire until her fingers clenched in his hair and her sex shuddered again and again and again. He was now as she had been. He was receptive in the dark, gazing into the night and seeing nothing but the dim shape of Jake's body as Jake moved to lie above him.

Jake stroked his cheek and trailed a finger across Renard's slightly parted lips before leaning down to kiss him. The kiss was slow, sensual, overlaid with a pulsing heat.

Renard reached up to hold Jake's face between his palms. His fingers slipped into Jake's soft hair as Jake moved to kiss the hollow of his throat and Renard's toes curled. "Jake." His voice was amused and slightly strained. "If you keep that up, I'm afraid I won't last much longer."

"Maybe I want to make you come." But Jake's grin was ragged, and his features were haggard with unfulfilled desire. "Hell, I want to make us both come."

Renard pushed at Jake's shoulder until he rolled gently onto his back, arms and legs splayed, eyes closed. A long shudder ran through Jake when Renard took his cock into his mouth, and Jake cried out as Renard suckled him. "Oh, God!" His fists clenched and unclenched at his sides as Renard worked him, drawing his cock deep into his throat. Renard reached up and slid two fingers into Jake's mouth, drew them out, and traced wet circles around Jake's hard nipples. "Oh, don't stop, don't stop…." Jake shuddered, fisting the sheets as Renard increased the speed and tenor. "I'm gonna come." He panted harshly, and Renard drew back, stroking him until Jake's face contorted and he grabbed Renard's wrist and cried out, spilling himself over the sheets and Renard's hand.

Jake moved toward him and kissed him, wrapping his hand around Renard's erection and sliding his palm slowly up and down the shaft. He deepened the kiss and worked Renard's cock slowly, in an agonizing rhythm up and down, up and down, until the moving ridge of pleasure struck Renard in the small of his back and throbbed through him, leaving him limp and powerless and spent.

"THE FIRST dead body I ever saw was a man murdered by his young wife in Marseilles. She'd quite beaten his head to pieces with an iron pot." Nicolas Renard turned his head on the pillow to glance at the man beside him. "You listening?"

"Uh-huh."

"Good. I rather thought that sleepy-eyed look was part of your regular demeanor, and I'm gratified to be proven right." Renard sighed. "I've seen all kinds of things in my years, Jake. People do terrible things to one another."

"Like somebody did to Yvette."

"Yes."

It was the middle of the night, or very early morning, and the searchlights swept now and then overhead, briefly illuminating their faces. "You know, Nicolas"—Jake Plenty tilted his head and gazed at the other man with affection—"naked, you look a lot younger."

"Is that so?" Renard rolled up on his elbow. "How old do you suppose I am, Jake?"

"Older than me." Jake shrugged. "Doesn't matter."

"Mmmm." Renard caressed Jake's face. "Strange how we keep ending up like this. It does rather rule out the possibility of coincidence."

"I don't know." Jake reached across Renard and retrieved his cigarettes from the nightstand. "Maybe some things are inevitable. Maybe we should have done this years ago. Hell, maybe we should have done this before we went over the top at Gallipoli. Would have made things a helluva lot easier on me, later on in the war."

"Yes, I suppose so." Renard accepted a lit cigarette. "You've never… you've never spoken about it. Your time there." He saw Jake's expression and held up a hand. "Not that I would expect that. No…." He was silent for a moment. "I will never forget the first time I caught a glimpse of you being led up the stairs by that Turk. You came blinking into the light like Lazarus restored to life."

"Oh, now you're the messiah." Jake reached for Renard's hand and held on. "There's nothing much to tell, Nicky. I went in. I came out."

*The pain can stop anytime, effendi. Just say the word. Perhaps you will say it soon enough to save your feet, eh? You will walk again?*

He shivered involuntarily and shoved the memory to the back of his mind where it belonged.

"I'm sorry," Renard murmured. "I should never have brought it up."

"Not your fault." Jake drew on his cigarette. "It got so that all the days were the same, one just blending into all the others. If

I complained too much about the food, they put me in a hole in the ground with a grating overhead…. There was this one guard, a big guy named Sadi. He used to stand up there and piss on me!" Jake laughed. "He used to… stand up there and piss down through the holes." His laughter faded into nothing. "I guess it ain't so funny after all." He examined the end of his cigarette; the red light of burning tobacco made strange patterns on his face. "Nicolas, why did you come after me? That day I got captured, we were shelled, and you and that other guy—what was his name?"

"Sabatin." Renard could see him as clear as day: a tall, thin man with sandy hair and a little moustache. "Louis Sabatin. He had the biggest feet I'd ever seen."

Jake nodded. "I keep thinking maybe it would have been better if I'd been gassed."

Renard shrugged. "Perhaps, although I don't recommend it." His fingers tightened on Jake's hand. "I blame myself."

"For me?"

Renard nodded. "Not that it made any difference, the… outcome. The Turks already knew, and by then it was too late. We tipped the war in our favor."

"Yeah." Jake drew a shaking breath. "I thought about you a lot when I was in the hole. I'd get these cramps in my legs like… Jesus God, like needles… and I'd think about me and you when we were on Corsica, doing our training, going out at night, getting drunk, and raising Cain. I had all these plans for what I was going to do when I got out." He crushed out his cigarette. "If I got out."

"I would never leave you in that place, Jacob." Renard pulled Jake into his arms. "It didn't matter to me what I had to do. You know, that was what they drilled into us."

"Yeah." Jake's voice sounded strange, even to himself. "Yeah, I remember that. Don't leave nobody behind. *Legio patria nostra* and all that."

"Katja would have killed me if I'd left you there." Renard sounded gently amused. "I think she would have bashed my head in with a cooking pot."

"She...." Jake cleared his throat. "Her... her tongue."

"Oh, she didn't need a tongue. That woman could harangue a man with a look alone." Renard smiled. "I loved her very much. She never told me much about it... next to nothing, really. Just that she was a White Russian and opposed the Bolsheviks. The remainder I put together on my own: the march across the lake, the... rest of it." One day Renard had brought home a newspaper with a story about the Bolsheviks, and it made Katja very angry. She had stabbed at the paper with her index finger and gestured at the root of her severed tongue until Renard understood. "She was adamant that we go and get you. Once word had come as to where you were, she insisted." A letter from Christophe Picard, posted from St. Petersburg and written in an obtuse and labored code. Even then, Picard had made connections for himself in the revolutionary underworld. Picard had met Renard and Katja at a crossroads: a fitting gesture, but then, Picard had always been fond of drama. "It was Picard who got us in there. I'd have never known where to even look, but he knew... he always knew."

Renard was talking to himself: Jake Plenty was sound asleep.


"THAT WAS a rather nice touch, asking to cash your chips first. You must have suspected you were going to your death." Christophe Picard gazed at the man sitting across from him: the bruises under Abaroa's eyes had faded somewhat, and now he merely looked like someone had tried to color him in with a charcoal pencil. His broken fingers were still taped, of course, but he was smoking a cigarette with the aplomb usually due a condemned man.

"I'd won two thousand francs. I wasn't going to leave it there." Abaroa smiled, a charming sort of dimpled smile.

"What I don't understand," Picard continued, "is why they stopped short of killing you."

Abaroa made a face. "You sound as if you regret it. Would you rather they had beaten me to death?"

Picard's face was blank, almost expressionless. He looked like a two-dimensional cutout rather than a man, or a figure that had been painted on a backdrop. "The Gestapo almost always carry out what they intend… I'm curious as to why they stopped. It's not such an unusual question."

"You sound like you don't trust me." It was said as gently as Frederik Abaroa said anything, but there was steel somewhere at the back of it. "And yet you came to Maarif looking for me, monsieur. I wonder why that is, hmm? What was it you said to me in France? *Don't kill him unless you absolutely have to, but I must have a visa.*" Abaroa leaned forward, his features taut. "Your orders, monsieur… your orders."

"It isn't you I don't trust." Picard shifted uncomfortably in his chair. He smiled, attempting levity, but there was a falseness in it, an expression hastily slapped on at the last minute in an effort to save face. "It's Monsieur Renard. After all, you were in his hands. It was Monsieur Renard who took charge of your arrest and interrogation. It was Monsieur Renard who managed to somehow spirit you safely away before the Gestapo killed you."

"Monsieur Renard is Free French, just as I am," Abaroa spat. "You know this. His remaining in Maarif as the *préfet* of police is just as risky to him as your position is to you."

"Ah, yes," Picard purred. "But his position is rather more lucrative than mine. He is close friends with the brothel owner, Jake Plenty. People say he's there every night. It appears they have some sort of—" Picard's long fingers played with a spent matchstick on the table. "—arrangement."

Abaroa's face hardened. "Do you feel guilty, Monsieur Picard? Is there perhaps something on your conscience?" He got up from the table, wandered over to a shuttered window, and spent some long moments gazing through the louvered slats at the desert beyond. "Do you know how much I hate this place? This Maarif? It's like a festering sore…. So many forlorn people crushed together inside so many square miles of sand and desperation…." He glanced at Picard sitting motionless behind him. "Nicolas Renard was your contact in Maarif. I was to get you a visa, and I did it. I don't see what the problem is, monsieur." Abaroa forced himself to breathe through the painful constriction of his damaged ribs. "You have secured your escape. This is the *fait accompli* you were hoping for. In a few days' time, you will be on your way to Portugal, freed at last from your worries. 'What a brave man he is, that Christophe Picard.' That is what people will say, no? 'How courageous he is.'"

"Stop it!" Picard rose from his chair, his fists clenched. "I hate the sound of your voice when you say that—when anyone says it. I have never wanted to be a hero. My God, the only heroes I know are dead men!" He turned so that he was in profile, gazing at the window but seeing nothing.

*It was*, Abaroa thought, *as if he expected someone to take his picture for the newspapers: THE HERO PICARD.*

"Only dead men." Abaroa's stomach clenched. "I was very nearly one of them."

"Frederik." Picard touched his shoulder gently, his face a mask of compassion and concern. "You should know me by now…. You should know I have never had anything in mind but your best interest."

"Mmm." Abaroa nodded. "It's just inconvenient that I survived the beating that should have killed me—is that it?" He tilted his head. "That's what I don't understand. You have what you wanted. The thing is done. Why bother yourself about trifles?"

"Because I can't help wondering what Nicolas Renard promised Danzig."

"Not you," Abaroa said bitterly. "Never fear. You're much too important for that. Give him some credit, Christophe—he does have some brains, despite what you might think."

"No one is disputing that." Picard didn't seem to know what to do with his hands. "It's how he uses them that worries me. Yes, as far as we know, he's abandoned his loyalties to Vichy, but can we really know?"

Abaroa stared at him. "Can anyone really know anyone else, Christophe? Perhaps you don't really know me." He drew a careful breath. "And perhaps I don't really know you."

Picard stood to go. "I'm grateful to you. And… proud of you, if that means anything, after all these years."

*Good God*, Abaroa thought, *he's still making speeches*. "Thank you," he said dryly.

"Don't let us part like this," Picard begged. "It's not you I'm worried about, can't you understand that? It's him—it's Renard! They didn't kill you, and I can't help but wonder what he promised them to make them stop." His expression cleared. "But, of course, you would have heard everything!" He seized Abaroa by the upper arms. "You must have heard what Renard said!" Picard shook Abaroa gently, heedless of the pain he was causing. "What did he say, Frederik? What was it?"

"Let go of me!" Abaroa wrenched away from him. "You madman! I was nearly unconscious! I was insensible with pain, and you're asking me this? Good God!" He rubbed his arms where Picard had grabbed him.

"I need to know if he betrayed me…. Please, Frederik… you must have heard something." He appeared to collapse a little inside his suit, and some of the color drained out of his already pale face. "I'm sorry," he said dully. "You have your papers now too. You can leave Maarif as soon as you like." He reached toward Abaroa but stopped just short of touching him. "If you ever remember… you will tell me, won't you? What Renard said?"

"If you're so worried," Abaroa said, "why not ask him yourself?"

Picard smiled tiredly. "He wouldn't tell me anything. I'm quite sure he despises me."


"As much as I'd love to stay, Jake—oh, thank you." Renard accepted the cup of coffee Jake passed him. He sipped at it while tying his tie. "As much as I've love to stay, I'd rather be at the préfecture when the rest of Maarif wakes up."

"How do you know it's not already awake?" Jake asked. He crawled back between the rumpled sheets, a cup cradled between his palms, a lit cigarette in his mouth.

"Don't be silly. You've been in the desert long enough to know the difference of that." Renard combed his hair into place, wondered whether the love bite on his throat was visible above his collar, then decided he didn't care. "I'm going out to the scene later this morning. I've had Andine and some of my men comb the place for evidence, but I'd rather have another look myself, just to refresh my memory." He gazed at Jake in the mirror. "You could come along if you'd like."

"Nah, I'd better stay here. You know, Nicolas, we spend too much time together and people are going to talk. How's it going to sound to Vichy if word gets out that you're...."

"A connoisseur of the carnal delights?" He stood and buckled on his Sam Browne belt. "My dear boy, you obviously forget that I'm French." Renard grinned. "I'm a man of diverse tastes."

"How come you've never bothered with my girls?"

Renard snapped open his revolver and spun the cylinder, snapped it shut again, and shoved it into his holster. "Jake, my dear, your girls are whores, and I've never been—" The realization of what he'd said hit him like a hammer. "I... my dear boy, please forgive me."

"Oh, it's all right." Jake's smile was brittle. "I'm not under any illusions here. Don't worry, Nicolas. I'm a big boy now."

The silence grew between them; Jake smoked and Renard fiddled with his belt. Predictably, Renard was the first to speak. "What I said was unconscionable. You know I would never... that is to say... I have never, ever thought of you that way." He dropped his head.

"You're just not as discerning when it comes to men as you are with women." Jake crushed out his cigarette. "It's shaping up to be a long war, Nicolas. If you and I can help each other pass the time, I don't mind."

"Is that what it is?" Renard went and sat on the bed. "Passing the time together?"

Jake reached up, pulled Renard down, and wrapped his arms around him. The kiss was long, slow, hot, and wet, and Renard groaned gently when Jake pulled away. "No regrets, Nicolas." If Jake's voice was husky with some unspent emotion, neither man was willing to mention it. "See you tonight?"

Renard shook his head, still mortified at his earlier faux pas. "Not tonight, no. I'm hoping to track down a decent pathologist today, and if I can find one, I'll want the autopsy done as soon as possible." He grinned. "But if you find you can't stay away, you know where I live…."

Jake laughed. "That sort of coy looks good on a girl. On you it looks ridiculous. Now get outta here."

Renard kissed him. "Good-bye, Jake."

"Don't get yourself shot or anything."


JAKE LAY back on the rumpled sheets, smiling to himself. He'd enjoyed last night, and he was pretty sure Nicolas had enjoyed it too. The older man was quite something in the sack—knew how to handle himself—but Jake had given as good as he got, and he'd got plenty. The first time was lightning fast, the kind of quick lay he always went for at the outset, but once they'd both gotten it out of their systems, things slowed down real nice, and they'd had a fine time wrecking the sheets. Hell, it had been a long time since he'd had anything of that quality between his sheets, and maybe he'd spend the rest of today smiling.


BY HALF past ten that morning, Nicolas Renard was well aware of the kinds of things that went on in Maarif, and few of them were good. A raging headache had begun over his right eye, the kind of aggravating pain that usually went along with complicated murder investigations. The search teams he'd left behind at the murder scene had turned up no more than the usual detritus: pebbles, a dead scorpion, a lump of partially chewed *qat* that could have belonged to just about anyone in Maarif.

He looked up from a pile of contradictory eyewitness reports as Andine appeared, bearing a coffee pot. "Is that for me?"

"Oui, monsieur." Andine set it down and poured for him. "I saw you rubbing your head, and I thought you might need a little something." He gestured with his chin at the stack of reports. "Anything?"

"Pfft." It was one of those noises that only the French can make with any efficacy. "Listen to this, Andine. 'I was walking my dog when I saw the young woman being pushed out of an automobile onto the ground. This was approximately two o'clock this morning.'"

"Two o'clock this morning." Andine's face was carefully expressionless. "*Eh bien*, at least some of the others, they can tell time?"

"Not really," Renard said. "Heard from the pathologist yet?"

"He says he will be here around four o'clock this afternoon. What time are you going out to the site?"

"I might as well go now," Renard said, "judging by the utter uselessness of what I'm doing here." He sipped some more of Andine's excellent coffee and rubbed his head.

"Did you… have a good night, *Monsieur le Préfet*?" Andine wasn't quite hovering.

"Guillaume, if there is something else you wish to ask me related to this investigation, by all means, have at it. Otherwise, bring my car round and have it waiting for me at the side door in five minutes. Is that clear?"

"But, monsieur—"

"I said, is that clear?" Renard didn't usually have to give a command twice. "Because, by God, lieutenant, if you should like to be reassigned to somewhere less hospitable than Maarif, I should be more than happy to effect your transfer."

"*Non*, monsieur." Andine ducked his head. "I will ready your car, monsieur."

"Good," Renard said. "Do that."


ABAROA'S CONVERSATION with Christophe Picard had left him feeling a little weak and sick, so he'd gone back upstairs to lie down. Captain Renard's house boy, Ali, was outside tending to something or other in the garden, and the house was very quiet. Abaroa lay back and let himself drift, his fatigue easily overcoming the pain in his hands and his body.

He dreamed he was in Algiers again. It was very late at night or perhaps very early, and he was alone, wandering down a street that looked faintly familiar, but at the same time was nowhere he had ever seen. His feet were bare, as they so often were in his early years, but it was warm, and he didn't mind. He had a few francs in his pocket, and he could buy something to eat from a street vendor if he wanted to fill his belly, perhaps even a kebab if he felt extravagant. He didn't have to go back to Qasim anymore—Christophe said that from now on, no one owned Frederik Abaroa, not even Qasim, and no one could make him do anything he didn't want to do. He no longer had to carry Qasim's firewood or put up with Qasim's insults, or the sudden and violent blows from Qasim's work-hardened hands. He was free.

*You know what I want you to do for me, Frederik?* Christophe Picard was younger in the dream, and his face was set in softer lines, as though he hadn't yet taken up the great worries that would from now on mark and erode his life. *It's something very special, Frederik, and you are the only one who can do it for me.*

*You know I'll do whatever it is you want,* Abaroa said. *I gave you my word, didn't I?*

*What did he tell them?* Picard asked. He came near and pressed a revolver into Abaroa's hands. *What did Renard tell them, to make the Germans stop beating you? Do you remember?*

*I don't know. I don't remember.*

*But you must remember! You must! This is nonsense!* And Christophe was holding on to Abaroa's upper arms and shaking him. Christophe was shaking him so hard that his teeth were coming loose.

Abaroa sat up with a gasp, sweating in the still air.

"So tell me." Jake Plenty drew on his cigarette, his expression cold and calculating. "Tell me what Renard said to them."


THE LIGHTS made Renard's eyes burn, or perhaps that was merely fatigue. He felt like he'd been up for twenty hours. This morning's visit to the scene of Yvette's murder seemed dim and faraway, as though it had happened in another country and to someone else. The cups of strong Moroccan coffee he'd had in lieu of supper did nothing to calm or soothe him—on the contrary, he started at shadows and felt entirely capable of leaping out of his own skin.

"Monsieur le Capitaine, the doctor, he is here." Andine leaned in to announce it.

"All right, I'm coming." His mouth quirked in private amusement. The last time he'd said those particular words had been under entirely different circumstances. "Tell him to start. I'll be there in a moment." He stepped into his private bathroom, undid his collar and tie, and splashed some water onto his burning face.

*Just like that…. Jesus, Nicolas…. Nicolas….* He groaned quietly, remembering. Who knew Jake Plenty could be so very passionate, and so responsive? Ah, well… if he ever managed to get Jake into bed again, it wouldn't be until well after this investigation had been completed. Some things couldn't be rushed.

He went absolutely still. Jake would have gone to see Abaroa, would have asked Abaroa questions about the interrogation and about him. Of course Abaroa didn't remember. He was nearly insensible, too far gone with pain and exhaustion to remember anything even if Renard had spoken aloud. But Renard wasn't that stupid. Rather, he was methodical and neat and liked to make sure all the ends were tied. It prevented nasty accidents later on. Of course, Abaroa wasn't going to tell Jake Plenty what Renard had said, the deal he had brokered with the Nazis. Abaroa was on his way to Portugal. Abaroa wasn't going to tell.

*Mais non*, Renard's reflection said. *He isn't going to tell Jake Plenty. Malheureusement, you are.*

He squinted into his own eyes, then leaned back to fasten his collar and tie. He checked his Sam Browne and adjusted the tilt of his hat. Jake Plenty didn't bother him. Renard had everything sewn up.

*You're a liar.*


"MONSIEUR LE capitaine, this is Doctor Morris. He is an Australian." Andine introduced them and ducked away. Apparently dead bodies made him queasy.

Morris was young, dark-haired, and handsome. He smiled as if contemplating something altogether more pleasant than an autopsy. "Captain Renard." The Australian accent was very strong, as though he'd just arrived.

"Doctor Morris. It's my pleasure." Renard shook his hand. "But what's an Australian doing in Maarif?"

"Oh, you know how it is," he said. "Everybody comes here eventually, isn't that right?" He grasped the edge of the sheet that lay over her face. "Are you ready?"

"Quite."

The sight of a corpse that had lain for days in an uncooled morgue was rather less than salutary. Renard was suddenly glad he'd had nothing to eat all day. The blood had pooled in her buttocks and heels, which was consistent with her having been found faceup. The flesh on the dorsal side of her body was dark purple, shading into black. Her abdomen had begun to bloat and turn green, and worst of all, there were tiny maggots wriggling from the horrible wound in her throat. "It's a shame what happens in the heat."

"It is indeed, Captain Renard." The waft of cigarette smoke cut neatly through the smell of Yvette's decomposing flesh. Aleksander Danzig stood in the doorway, looking like he'd been hung up to dry. "You seem surprised to see me, captain. Perhaps you thought I had returned to Berlin?"

"Not at all, major." Renard arranged his face into a more suitable expression, even though his heart was slamming into his ribs with fright. "I had hoped we might have a drink together before you left, perhaps even dinner."

Morris stood back from the corpse, the blue eyes above his mask wide with shock. "I beg your pardon… should I continue?" He looked from Renard to Danzig and back again. "If now is inconvenient…."

*He is*, Renard thought, *being wonderfully diplomatic about it, considering that Danzig is probably the first Nazi he's ever seen up close.* "Not at all, my dear boy. Go on with your work. The major and I will observe from over here." Privately, he enjoyed the expression of disgust on Danzig's face. It pleased him to know there was something even Danzig found repulsive. "Quite all right, major? I realize the air in here is quite close."

"No, it is fine. We Germans must learn to adapt to all circumstances. The smell of death is a natural part of war." He nodded at Morris. "Carry on, young man." He fetched out his handkerchief and held it to his nose. "She was found in the souk, correct?"

*You've been busy.* "Yes, major. She had been there awhile. The throat wound is quite decomposed."

"She was a whore, was she not? In Germany, we take measures to remove such women before they can contaminate us."

*And that's why Stussel was killed in Jake Plenty's brothel.* "Quite so, major. Quite so."

"I am very interested in meeting this Jake Plenty." Danzig leaned over Renard's shoulder and peered down at the corpse. "Perhaps tomorrow evening? In the—"

"Brothel." Renard forced himself to sound pleasant. "The name of the place is Paradise, and it is a brothel, major. If you are interested in meeting Jake, the very best time to do that is around eleven. I'm afraid he doesn't appear until later in the day. His barman, Piet, will see to it that you are furnished with refreshments."

"Until tomorrow night, then." Danzig bowed and stepped out into the night.

Renard heard a car start up and drive off. Only then did he allow himself to relax. "Right, er, Doctor Morris, please carry on. I apologize for the interruption." Renard avoided looking at Yvette's face. It was too much, even for him. Most of the murder victims that came his way were unknowns, poor bastards who'd wandered into Maarif looking for the same things as the rest of them and who ended up bashed in the head or knifed in some dark place and forgotten. There were scores of nameless foreigners buried in shallow graves of sand or under makeshift rocky cairns in the desert. But Renard didn't know them personally. It was jarring, to say the least.

"Let's get it over with. I want to know if anything besides that wound killed her." He stood back and watched as the pathologist cut and sliced, carved and weighed. The whole scene had a surreal flavor to it and felt like something happening to someone else. He leaned his head back against the wall, which was cooler than the rest of the room because it was night, and night was the best time to perform an autopsy, but it didn't matter because Jake Plenty would find out anyway. Jake always found out everything. There was no keeping anything from the man.

"Captain?"

Renard blinked himself awake. The sodium lights hissed above them, far too bright, and there was music coming from somewhere, the sound of a tinny piano. He rubbed his eyes. "What is it?"

"You were right. It's the wound in her throat that did her in. She bled to death." Morris looked almost apologetic. "I didn't find anything else."

Renard digested this in silence for a moment. "Right." He nodded to himself. "Thank you, doctor. You've been very helpful." He stumbled out into the night, forcing himself to breathe deeply. The corpse stench lingered in his nostrils, seemed to insinuate itself into his clothes, his skin. He felt weak, dizzy. He supported himself against the side of a building until the fit passed.

Normally Renard would have taken his car, but tonight he felt like walking. The stench of the police morgue clung to his hands, his clothes, and the lingering fetor of decomposition seemed to have been permanently seared into his nostrils. The warm night air of Maarif—even choked with the stench from a dozen uncovered drains—seemed to chase the smell away. He was violently unsettled by the things he had seen. This was not his first autopsy, and he knew it would not be his last, but Renard never really got used to seeing dead people. He supposed in some circles that could be considered a weakness, and perhaps there were some who would disparage him for his lack of stomach, but he couldn't help it. It was always a shock to see what had once been a person become nothing more than a chilly slab of flesh.

*What are you waiting for? Stab him with your bayonet! Goddammit, Renard, the Turks are coming! Do it!*

The man had been absurdly young—younger even than Renard—and gibbering in fright. There was a dark stain on the front of his uniform trousers where he'd pissed himself. He held his hands out in front of him and shouted something Renard didn't understand, and Renard knew he had to kill him, that the man could not be allowed to live, but something held him rooted to the ground.

Jake Plenty had come up behind him, saw the man on the ground, and took out his revolver.

Renard had argued with him: *No, don't do it…. We'll tie him up…. We can tie him up and just leave him here, we can….*

The pistol barked once, twice, and the Turk's body jumped and then lay still. *Come on.* Jake hauled him by the arm. *We don't have time to stand here crying over him.*

"Well, Nicolas, whatta ya know? Fancy meeting you here." Jake took the cigarette from his mouth and tossed it on the ground. "You look like you've seen a ghost."

"No." Renard took some deep breaths. "I've just come from the autopsy."

"And?"

"The wound in her throat…." Renard straightened. "My theory is that she was slashed and left to die… slowly. It's the sort of killing that usually points to a grudge." He fumbled in his uniform tunic for a cigarette and lit it with shaking fingers. "But what are you doing? We've a curfew in Maarif, you know that. And it's well after midnight." He drew on his cigarette with something like gratitude. "Major Danzig paid us a little visit over at the police station. He says he wants to meet you, tomorrow night at Paradise."

"If it's well after midnight, maybe we better both get inside. Otherwise, you'll have to fine me and yourself too. Come on." Jake took him by the arm and steered him toward Paradise.

Renard was at once grateful for the physical support—he was still wobbly in the knees—and irritated. "You needn't tow me around."

Jake laughed, but it wasn't a nice laugh. It wasn't the sort of laugh Renard had become used to hearing, but the other kind. "Oh, I think I'd better. See, you and me need to have a talk, Nicolas." Jake yanked open the door and propelled him inside. "The sooner the better." The inside of the brothel was dark. Jake walked Renard to the bar and pushed him none too gently onto a stool. "Frederik Abaroa will soon be leaving Maarif."

"How very perceptive you are, Jake." Renard rubbed his forehead.

"And he's not leaving in a box." Jake sat on the stool opposite and stared at him.

Their faces were so close together that Renard could have leaned across and kissed him, if he dared. He didn't. "No, he's leaving more or less whole. How very fortunate."

"I like you, Nicolas...."

Naked bodies sliding together, slick with sweat and body fluids. Jake's beautiful mouth murmuring, whispering, *I love you, I love you.* Renard blinked. Now was hardly the time to remember selected highlights from their night together. "And I like you, dear boy."

"But you're a goddamn liar, and I've had enough of it."

A dangerous emotion throbbed under the surface of Renard's skin. "Careful, Jake."

"Who did you promise Danzig? I might play dumb now and again, but I'm not stupid, and I know you told him something, promised him somebody. Who was it? Christophe Picard?"

"Don't be absurd. If Danzig wanted to take Salazar, he could have done it the first night Salazar appeared in Maarif. Do you think Danzig didn't realize Salazar was coming?"

"Who was it? Maybe you planned to turn Abaroa over to them all along. Maybe if Salazar didn't roll over, you figured you'd give them Abaroa and they'd get the information they wanted."

Renard's expression hardened and he stood. "Why do you think I'd do that, Jake? Do you think everybody breaks under torture—just because you did?"

*Just say it, effendi... say it and all this will be over.... We will let you sleep.... We have prepared a nice, cozy bed for you, see? Over there, a nice, cozy bed. You can lie down and sleep as long as you like. You know what we want. Just say it. How many troops will the Allies be landing at Gallipoli?*

*I don't know. God, please leave me alone.*

*The huge Turk's monstrous hands tightened on his left foot, crushing the small bones of his toes, and Jake Plenty screamed. He screamed and screamed until his ears were filled with the sound of his own screaming, and then the world went dark.*

"Who was it?" Jake's heart hammered against his ribs. "What deal did you make with that devil, Nicolas? Did you promise them Abaroa?"

Renard's gut churned. "No," he said quietly, "I promised them you."

Jake's expression of disbelief was almost comical. And then his face closed down. "You son of a bitch," he said—and hit Renard as hard as he could.

The blow struck Renard square in the face and threw him backward onto the floor. For a moment he flirted with unconsciousness while the room whirled around him. He forced himself onto his hands and knees and from there onto his feet. He staggered outside and vomited his guts beside the front door of Paradise.

# CHAPTER
# SIX

THE NIGHT Frederik Abaroa left for Portugal, the airfield was as dark as God and Nicolas Renard could make it. All day long, Abaroa had lain in wait at Renard's house, sweating through a violent fear that manifested itself as stomach cramps and rolling chills. By nightfall, he was exhausted. Around six, Ali brought food on a tray, but Abaroa could eat nothing. He pushed the food around on the plate and drank the wine and sat back on his bed to smoke a cigarette. His conversation with Jake Plenty replayed itself in his head, unbidden.

*What did he tell them, to make them stop beating you? Come on, Abaroa, you're the only one who knows.* Jake had walked back and forth, back and forth, smoking ceaselessly.

It felt to Abaroa like another interrogation. And he didn't have the information Plenty wanted—as he'd told Christophe Picard, he'd been close to unconsciousness by the time Renard managed to step in and stop the beating. All he knew was that it had stopped.

*Lucky for you,* Jake said. His eyes were cold. Clearly he didn't believe a word of it, but there was nothing he could do about it.

Abaroa had been instructed to wait by the front door—the house was far enough away from the center of Maarif that the search lights didn't touch it. He'd packed a few things in a bag: a change of clothes, his passport, his exit visa. He had a little money. He needed nothing else.

At half past eleven, a car drove up, and Guillaume Andine got out. "Get in," Andine said. He helped Abaroa into the backseat and slammed the door.

"Where is Captain Renard?" Abaroa asked. "He said he would be here to see me off."

"He is busy with the coroner," Andine replied, "and he said to tell you it's better if you and he are not seen together." He handed Abaroa a folded slip of paper. "He told me to give you this."

*My dear boy*, it read in Renard's tidy pen, *give my regards to our dear cousins in the north. I shall see you when I see you.* It was more than Abaroa had expected, less than he had hoped. Somehow, working all these long months at Renard's side, he had expected a more emotional send-off. But Andine was right: Renard was needed elsewhere, and it wouldn't do for Renard to be seen with Abaroa, just in case something went wrong, as it was wont to do in situations exactly like this.

At precisely midnight, Abaroa's plane lifted off for Lisbon by way of Oran—courtesy of an ersatz flight plan that crisscrossed nearly the whole of North Africa—and a providentially heavy cloud cover. Abaroa leaned forward and gazed out of the window. "*Adieu, Maarif.*" All things considered, he had accomplished exactly what his masters had sent him to do.


NICOLAS RENARD had been trying to sleep for several hours, without success. He wandered in and out of his bedroom, which seemed empty now that Frederik Abaroa had been spirited away to safety. One more flight to Lisbon, one more agony of waiting, and Christophe Picard would be safe. Perhaps then Renard might be able to rest, but he wasn't counting on it. The side of his face where Jake Plenty had hit him throbbed in time to the beat of his heart, and his stomach muscles were sore from vomiting.

It wasn't so much to do with Jake Plenty's fist or the guilt he felt at throwing Jake's past at him. It didn't even have much to do with the knowledge that he had let Jake down and would probably never get another chance to redeem himself. It had to do with Danzig. Of course… these days everything had to do with Danzig.

*Not like that, Captain Renard.... I want you on your knees.*

Renard shuddered, remembering. Some things were too horrible for words and should never be recalled to memory. How interesting that Danzig, as an instrument of the Third Reich, had stooped to violent sodomy to make Renard understand. It was almost ironic. If only the problem of Danzig could be solved by putting him on a plane—or pushing him out of one.

Renard wandered back into his bedroom and sat on the bed. Ali had changed the linens, the pillows were fluffed, and Renard's favorite robe was laid across the bedroom chair. The windows were open to the night breeze, and a selection of aromatic perfumes wafted into the air from the little *oud* burner on the dresser. Renard stripped off his clothes, hung his uniform up, and laid his shoes side by side next to the wall. He thought about putting them out for Ali to polish, but he hated doing that. It implied Ali was merely a servant, and Renard knew the difference, even if Ali didn't. He would have to tell Ali someday—someone should. It was better to know precisely where one stood in the scheme of things than to be forever living under a misunderstanding.

There was a photograph propped against the base of the bedside lamp showing a very young Frederik Abaroa standing next to Christophe Picard, both of them squinting into the sun. Renard picked it up. Abaroa was dressed in a motley assortment of rags, and he was barefoot. Picard looked the same as always: expressionless and stoic.

"Born a hero, weren't you?" Renard murmured.

"Sorry, was there something?" Ali appeared in the doorway. *"Mon capitaine?"*

"No, my dear boy, that's quite all right. You can run along to bed now." Renard set his glass on the nightstand beside the bed. He wouldn't sleep—he knew he wouldn't sleep. He might never sleep again. Perhaps he should ask Ali to prepare a pipe… no. It was getting to be too much of a habit for him, and he always paid dearly for it the next morning.

A woman was dead, an innocent woman who had never done anything to anyone, and it was Renard's job—no, it was his duty—to find her killer and bring him in. Thus far he had formed no theories and had deliberately avoided speculating on who might have had reason to kill her. Of course, the tenet of reason often had nothing at all to do with why killers killed. Renard knew this. For some, it was sport; for others, pleasure. Some years ago, before the war, he had been called to the house of a respectable married couple in one of the more affluent suburbs of Paris. Their teenage son had been found hanging by his neck in his bedroom closet, quite thoroughly dead. They suspected he had been murdered, and he had. The construction and location of the knot on his makeshift noose, however, indicated he had tied it himself, and the lack of a suicide note or any other indication led Renard to suspect that the boy might have been experimenting with a dangerous sort of solitary pleasure.

Renard had met the other kind of killer too, the ones for whom killing was a sport akin to big-game hunting, albeit with human prey. The whole world was their hunting ground, and they were so adept at masking their true natures that they could exist for years or even decades and escape detection by blending into the greater population.

In Tangiers, Renard had come dangerously close to this sort—a young woman who had presented herself at the police station, wanting to report her older brother missing. She was a thin, lackluster creature, with pale hair, pale eyes and lips, and a trembling voice. Her hand when Renard shook it felt dry and papery. A good gust of wind would have surely blown her over. She inquired whether someone could help her find her brother and gave a thorough description of him, even helped to make a sketch of him for the police to circulate. When she left, she took one of Renard's cards with her but declined the offer of a ride home and departed the station bravely stifling her sobs into a handkerchief. When she was apprehended, Renard's men found the corpses of six people hidden in a cellar underneath her house and dried blood under her fingernails. Renard didn't bother asking why. He knew.

He turned off the light, arranged the pillow under his head, and lay down. The house was absolutely silent, and even the smallest sounds were audible through the open window. The fluting call of some lonely night bird throbbed out into the darkness and was gone. A breeze lifted the window curtains and let them drop. Renard shifted his tired body in the bed and waited for sleep to come but knew it wouldn't—not yet, and maybe not for a while.

His thoughts turned to Frederik Abaroa. Renard had instructed Andine well in advance of Abaroa's exodus. *Don't go by a direct route. Danzig will be watching for that. Take the old road through the Thieves' Quarter, and dress in your ordinary clothes. Put him on the plane, and don't waste any time for tender good-byes, do you hear me? Abaroa is strong, but if Danzig gets a hold of him, he'll make sure that Frederik spills everything he knows.*

He had sworn Andine to secrecy. Renard had trusted no one with the details, not even Jake, and it was just as well. Jake had the answer he wanted, the only answer he would ever accept, and now that pleasant little interlude was over. *Perhaps*, Renard thought, *it was just as well.*

It was difficult to regret a mistake one had not yet made.


"*Mon capitaine*, the autopsy report has been filed here…." Lt. Andine stopped short as Renard, standing at the filing cabinet, turned around. "Mon Dieu," he murmured.

One side of Renard's face was practically covered by a huge, dark bruise, and his bottom lip was puffed and swollen. He looked worse this morning than he had the night before. The damage Jake's fist had done seemed determined to spread itself across Renard's features, announcing the injury to the world.

The palais de justice was busier than usual this morning, crammed with irate citizens and émigrés alike, all equally outraged, victims of some gross miscarriage of justice. A shipment of American cigarettes had gone missing from the quay, probably stolen by black marketers and even now being distributed around Maarif for the sorts of tidy sums such merchandise commanded. A local nightclub owner ferrying a load of booze across the river had been rammed from behind by person or persons unknown and was demanding that someone do something about it. The pretty teenage daughter of some exiled Maltese dignitary had been groped and "interfered with" in the street. An elderly Englishwoman and her superannuated sister had obscenities shouted at them by three youths in a car. Every telephone in the place was ringing off its hook, and several people were vociferously complaining about the heat in the anteroom.

Renard's head felt like it would burst.

"No." Renard shut his office door. "Not God. At least, not this time. No, this time it was Monsieur Jake."

"Monsieur Jake did that to your face?" Andine was incredulous but hardly stupid. In matters such as these, he was nearly a savant. "He must really hate you."

"Yes," Renard agreed, "I think he must."

"And Monsieur Christophe Picard is here to see you, capitaine."

Renard smiled bitterly. "My morning just gets better and better. Show him in, Andine."

"Captain Renard, I apologize…." Picard stopped short. Renard let him look his fill. "An accident?"

"You could call Monsieur Jake an accident." Renard gestured to a chair. "Please, have a seat. What can I do for you this morning, Monsieur Picard?" He wasn't in the mood for talk, and especially not with Christophe Picard. The only thing he wanted to do was crawl under his desk and die.

"I wanted to talk to you about the plane to Lisbon," Picard said.

Renard held up one hand as Andine came in and laid some papers on the desk. "Not here." He waited until the lieutenant had left. "We don't discuss such things in my office, Monsieur Picard.

Come and see me later, after hours, hmm? Come and see me in…." He drew a painful breath. "…in that little tearoom on the eastern side of the souk. I rather think I won't be welcome in Jake's Paradise for the foreseeable future."

"So what happened? To make him hit you?"

Renard's mouth twitched. "I gave him some information."

Picard lit a cigarette and blew a long plume of smoke into the air. "I'd think that was a good thing."

"Oh no, not in this case. In this case, it wasn't the sort of information he wanted to hear." Renard reached for the stack of papers Andine had left and made a show of paging through them.

"I am curious about one thing, Captain Renard."

"And what is that, monsieur?" Renard refused to meet his eyes. He didn't need the disapproval he almost certainly would see in Christophe Picard's gaze.

"Surely you should complain." Picard shrugged. "To someone. The administration in Vichy, perhaps."

Renard stared at him. "I beg your pardon? Because of Jake?"

"No." Picard shook his head. His gaze was lowered so Renard couldn't see his eyes. "You see, I was in a concentration camp, Monsieur Renard, as you know—Drancy, to be precise. Major Danzig was a frequent visitor to our… humble abode." He drew on his cigarette, his expression carefully aloof. "Like a great many of his stripe, he enjoys humiliation… enjoys it rather too much, if you take my meaning."

*Not that way, Captain Renard…. I want you on your knees.* "Yes, as fascinating as this is, Monsieur Picard, was there anything of importance? We are so very busy today—murder investigation, I'm sure you've heard." Renard got up from the desk and turned to the filing cabinet, turning his back to Christophe Picard.

"Does Jake know what you did? To save Abaroa, I mean."

"I'm sure I don't know what you're talking about," Renard replied. He'd intended it to sound airy and unconcerned, but it sounded wretched, like he was strangling. He looked up, and Picard was standing by his side, almost looming over him. "Good God," Renard cried, "what do you want?"

"When I was in the internment camp," Picard said, "Danzig enjoyed making surprise visits." He drew a breath. "One day he summoned the man who occupied the bunk next to mine. He was gone a long time. Danzig wanted to know what this man knew about the Resistance in Romania, the underground movement there. This man returned on his hands and knees, unable to even crawl. For three days he lay on his belly in his bunk, insensible. I wondered what Danzig had done to him...." Picard drew on his cigarette. A muscle at the corner of his eye twitched. "Then one night Danzig sent for me, and I found out." He met Renard's gaze, and Renard felt as if his soul were crumbling. "He didn't force me," Renard whispered.

"Yes, he did. Perhaps he was even civilized about it."

Andine knocked on the door and stuck his head in. "Captain, there is an urgent message for you. It just came by courier. Shall I...?" He indicated Picard by a look.

"Oh, yes," Renard said, "by all means. Mr. Picard and I were quite finished with our little talk."

Picard rose. "Ten o'clock? The tearoom in the souk... or would you prefer Jake's brothel?"

"That big doorman of his probably has orders to snap my neck like a chicken. Have you thought of that?" Renard made a face. "And might I add, Major Danzig most probably has plans to visit Paradise himself tonight. You are playing it a bit close, aren't you?"

"Sometimes one has to risk it. Let us meet there. We will be... hiding in plain sight. If Major Danzig wishes to speak to me...." Picard shrugged.

*For Christ's sake*, Renard thought, *the man's an idiot.*

Picard laid a hand on his shoulder, but only for a moment. "If Frederik Abaroa knew the whole of what you have done for him—"

"Yes, but he isn't going to find out," Renard snapped, "is he?"

"You're a strange man, Captain Renard."

"So I've been told." Renard turned away, effectively dismissing him. "Good day, Mr. Picard." He waited till Picard had gone before reading the message: two typed lines on a sheet of paper. Hardly worth the trip. *I know what happened to the girl. Meet me at the far edge of the souk at twelve.*

*Sacré nom de Dieu.*

Unwittingly, Renard had turned to face the mirror. He gazed at himself for a long moment. "And you'll go, won't you? Because you really are that foolish." The message could be anything, but Renard wasn't stupid enough to think it genuine—he'd been here before. As a young policeman in Marseilles, he'd worked a serial murder case involving a man who liked to chop off his victim's little fingers as a souvenir. One day a message had arrived at the police station: he was tired of running and wanted to come in, he said. He was ready to give himself up. He'd even—Renard smirked, remembering—asked for a priest. Renard had taken two gendarmes and gone to meet him at the prearranged rendezvous, a deserted alley by the side of an old church. But the killer wasn't stupid. He'd come heavily armed, and when Renard finally managed to subdue him, the two gendarmes were dead, as was the killer, and Renard was bleeding from a bullet wound in his jaw.

Yes, he'd go. But he wouldn't put any of his men in harm's way this time. He took out his revolver, spun the chamber, and snapped it shut. No, this time he would go alone.

# CHAPTER
# SEVEN

WHEN RENARD approached Paradise that evening, Jake was standing by the front door, smoking a cigarette. Although he appeared to be watching the street, his gaze was faraway and inward. He looked like a man with a great deal on his mind.

Renard moved to stand beside him. "Anything I can do?"

"Hello, Nicky." Jake nodded at the minaret of the great mosque, silhouetted against the sky. "Nicolas, do you believe in God?"

"Do I believe in God?" Renard pondered for a moment. "Well, I was raised a Catholic, like most Frenchmen…." He paused to light a cigarette. "No, Jake. I don't believe I do." His gaze, like Jake's, was drawn to the mosque. "That's a pretty piece of architecture. You know, that's something I've always admired about the Arabs. Damned clever bastards, every one of them. Between them and the Chinese, they invented just about everything." He tilted a look at Jake. "Why the somber turn of mind?"

Jake hadn't mentioned their previous altercation, and Renard wasn't going to. That meant it was something else.

"Nothing. Well, nothing much. I've been thinking about Christophe Picard." But instead of continuing the conversation, he motioned to Renard to follow him inside. "Come on, I'll buy you a drink."

They threaded their way through the crowded dance floor and up to the bar, which was already thronged three deep. Piet shuttled bottles and glasses back and forth with lightning alacrity while white-jacketed waiters came and went from the serving station. They bore away trays heavily laden with all manner of liquid refreshment.

"Piet, pour me one, would you? And one for Captain Renard."

"Right away, Mr. Jake! I will do it." Piet fetched glasses and made a couple of quick motions at the spirit optics mounted on the wall behind the bar. "Here you are." He nodded to Renard. "Enjoy."

"Come on, Nicolas, let's sit down. Might as well meet my doom in comfort." Jake led him to a table near the back. "When did Major Danzig say he was coming?"

"He didn't." Renard tasted his drink—too much scotch, not nearly enough soda. "I don't believe he likes me," he murmured.

"Who? Danzig?"

"Your barman."

"Nicolas, do you think Danzig knows—?"

"No."

"You didn't even let me explain."

Renard scanned the crowd for a Nazi uniform. "What Danzig knows you can fit into a very small thimble. That's precisely why he's here. Abaroa was right: North Africa is important in this war, and it's about to get a whole lot more important. Danzig and his cronies are here to pick up information."

"What about Abaroa?"

Renard tapped ash off his cigarette in an effort to appear casual. "He's here." Danzig and his little band of sycophants appeared in the doorway and gazed around them, watching the dancing couples with an expression of faint superiority.

"Oh, look at that," Jake smirked. "Or maybe they do it different in Berlin." He straightened his tie and rose from the table. "Time to call out a welcoming committee."

"Sit down." Renard snatched his wrist. "Please." Renard waved Danzig over. "Major! How nice to see you again. I don't believe you've met Mr. Jacob Plenty. He is the owner of Paradise."

"Is that what you call it? Paradise?" Danzig offered Jake a cool, dry hand and sat. His acolytes arranged themselves around the table. "I would have thought a less salutary title might be more in order." Danzig was dressed in white in deference to the desert heat, and his graying hair was combed straight back over his head and glistened with pomade. The blond man—the one who had carried his suitcases at the airport that day—was similarly attired. Even his hair was parted in the same fashion as Danzig's. As Renard watched, the blond man took out an embossed gold case, offered Danzig a cigarette, and lit it for him.

Danzig was all business. "Mr. Plenty, you are an American?"

The band had just struck up "Bounce Me, Brother," and couples all over the floor were beginning to swing it out. A redheaded man went up the stairs with Rolande, her hand firmly holding his elbow in case he might be thinking of escape, and Celeste, the little blonde dancer, was sitting in the lap of a darkly handsome American, giggling as he whispered into her ear.

"Yeah, originally. I haven't been back there in a while."

"Mmm. And you have been in Morocco how long?"

Jake tensed, and Renard reached out to lay his foot over Jake's, an unspoken warning. Abaroa was away, it was true, but Christophe Picard was still at large somewhere in Maarif, and, Renard reminded himself, stupid and self-sacrificing enough to stand up and introduce himself to Danzig, if he felt like it. Until Picard was on a plane to Portugal, there was absolutely nothing Jake or Renard could take for granted.

"Oh, I couldn't really say for sure, major." Jake pulled at his earlobe, a sure sign that he was becoming annoyed. "I've been kicked around a bit. I'm sure you know how it is."

The blond man glared at Jake. "What exactly do you mean by this? Are you insulting the major?" He stood so quickly that the glasses on the table rattled. "I will see you outside, sir!"

"Stop that!" Danzig slammed his fist into the table. "Damn you!" He glared at the other man, who sat down and sullenly smoked his cigarette.

*It should have a nipple on it*, Jake reflected, *considering....*

"Yes," Danzig continued, "I do understand. The war takes its toll on us all. So, before the war, you were in the French Foreign Legion, were you not?"

"Jake and I were in the Légion etrangère together," Renard put in. He glanced up as Piet appeared at the table, bearing a bottle of Veuve Cliquot and a tray of glasses. "Ah, Piet! How adept you are at anticipating our needs." He lifted the bottle and examined the label. "Yes, this will do nicely. Put it on my bill."

"Champagne," Danzig murmured. "This is rather extravagant, Mr. Plenty. Business must be very good."

Jake's forehead creased. "Oh, I didn't order that, major. I've always got my eye on the bottom line. I don't know where it came from. Piet!" He motioned to the barman.

"You don't need to bother your barman, Monsieur Jake. It was I who ordered the champagne. I believe it is time I introduced myself to your… guests."

Jake's gaze was drawn to the sound of that voice, and his mouth went dry as the Sahara. "Jesus Christ…." *You idiot. You goddamn idiot.*

He smiled. "I am Christophe Picard. You perhaps know me as Salazar."

"Mr. Picard." Danzig rose from the table and shook Picard's hand. "I cannot tell you what a consummate pleasure it is to finally meet you. I have been chasing you all over Europe." He indicated a chair to his right. "Will you join us?"

"Not at all, monsieur. I am afraid I cannot stay. I merely wanted to welcome you to Maarif and to promise you that my intentions here are the same as everyone else who comes to Maarif."

Danzig's expression hardened. "Which is?"

"To leave."

"Mr. Picard, let me assure you, if you attempt to leave Maarif illegally, my men will have you shot. Any attempt to leave by regular channels, of course, will meet with failure. You cannot escape. However, I will allow you to remain at large while I conclude my investigation."

"Oh." Picard smiled. "How very generous of you." He turned as a woman came to stand beside him. "There you are, my dear. I hope I didn't keep you waiting too long?"

Jake Plenty's face felt frozen. There had been no woman. Picard had arrived in Maarif on his own, wounded and very much in need of Jake's protection. What the hell was this? What kind of game was Picard playing? And then he remembered how, when he'd gone to Picard's hotel, Picard had repeatedly asked if anyone had called for him or left a message. Obviously, this was who he'd meant.

"Not at all, my dear."

Picard drew her to his side. She was young, not more than twenty-five, and luminously beautiful. Her light brown hair gleamed under the brothel's lights, and her green eyes were intelligent and full of keen discernment. She was dressed simply, but elegantly, in a long evening skirt and a silk blouse. She wore no flowers or jewelry. "Gentlemen, might I present my wife, Maartje."

Jake turned to Renard, white to the lips. "Your wife." He clenched his shaking hands into fists. "Your wife."

"And now, gentlemen, I hope you enjoy your champagne." Picard bowed. "Good night."

Jake bolted out of his chair and charged after Picard, nearly knocking over a large man with pointy, waxed moustaches who was dancing with a tall African girl from Brazzaville, one of Jake's most recent acquisitions. Jake caught Picard by the shoulder and spun him around. "What the hell do you think you're doing? Waltzing in here and showing yourself off! What are you, off your nut?"

"Jake, this is not the place."

Maartje clutched at Picard's arm. "Christophe, please. You at least owe him an explanation. This has to be a terrible shock for him."

Jake sneered. "I don't want any explanation." He glanced around and lowered his voice. "I risk my neck…. Frederik Abaroa nearly died, and Renard could end up in front of a firing squad, and you come in here like you own the place, order a bottle of champagne, and introduce us to your wife? What's she even doing here, and since we're on the subject, did you bring her to Maarif in your suitcase?"

Picard turned. "Marta, perhaps you can wait for me at the hotel, yes?" He kissed her cheek and drew her briefly to his side, and then she was gone, slipping through the crowd and out the door.

Jake watched her nod good night to the doorman, Emil. "She's a nice girl, your wife. Does she know about you?"

Picard took Jake's elbow and drew him to a table in an alcove, out of Danzig's line of sight. "It would take longer than I have right now to explain. Marta is my wife, really. We have been married for two years. Her father was a Resistance fighter who was killed in the early days of the war. I promised her father that I would look after her."

"So that's what it is." Jake's gut twisted itself into knots and his face felt hot. "Taking care of her. Yeah. That's what it looks like."

"Jake, I don't have much time. Marta just arrived here this morning. She is very important to my work."

"Yeah, your work." Jake nodded. "We can't forget about that. Who's gonna save the world if you don't, huh?" The bitterness rose in his throat and choked him, and he couldn't understand for the life of him why he was feeling this way. Picard shouldn't mean anything to him; all that was over years ago, and he had no right to be jealous. The girl had looked at Picard with such pride and such love, all of it right there shining in her beautiful eyes, that it made Jake sick with envy to see it. "Get out of here," he said, "before you get us all killed."

Renard was alone at the table when Jake returned. "You've made Major Danzig a very happy man." He poured a little of the Veuve Cliquot and pushed the glass across the table to Jake. "He's found precisely what he was looking for." He gazed at Jake speculatively. "Any idea where Our Fearless Hero has gone?"

"No." Jake buried his anguish in the wine glass. "No, and I don't give a damn either."

Renard's eyes narrowed, and when he spoke, his voice was harsh. "You had better give a damn. Abaroa had the means to get

Picard out of Maarif. Now find this mystery object so I can get him on a plane." He looked up as Piet came over to their table. "Monsieur Jake and I are busy. What is it?"

"Monsieur Jake, it is Lizbeth. You had better come and take care of it."

"What the hell is it now?" Jake stood angrily. "Can't I leave anything alone for a second without the whole damn works going to the devil?"

He left the table, Renard in tow, and followed the barman up the stairs to where the girls' rooms were. Lizbeth, a dark-haired sylph with a narrow waist and the sort of curvy hips that most men associated with Eastern odalisques, was sitting fully clothed on her bed, weeping into a handkerchief, while a red-faced, very irate German in full uniform paced the corridor outside, cursing softly to himself.

Jake slipped into the room. "What's the problem here? Lizzie, did that guy do something to you?"

The German pushed his way past Jake. "She refuses. She will not let me touch her. I offer her good money, and no. She will not."

Jake jerked his chin at the German officer. "Piet, get him out of here." He took Lizbeth's hands in his. "Can you tell me about it? You maybe don't feel well? You want me to get the doctor for you?"

"Jake, leave the girl alone." Renard hovered in the doorway. "She's unwell."

"No, monsieur, I am not." She crushed the handkerchief between her fists. "I promised him. I promised him that I would… I would keep it safe."

"Keep what safe, baby?" Jake reached out and daubed away the tears with his fingers. "If you got troubles, you know you can tell me."

"He said… he said he trusted me. He said to keep it until…." She drew a shaking breath, hiccoughing on a sob, and fell silent.

Jake stood, drew Renard into the room, and closed the door. "Tell me." He sat next to the shivering girl and drew her into his arms. "It's quite all right."

She leaned toward him and whispered something into his ear.

Jake stiffened, and his eyes grew dark. He was fairly vibrating with barely repressed excitement. He looked up at Renard and shook his head. "Whatta you know?" he breathed, and there was a little laughter in it. "Whatta you know about that...." He patted Lizbeth's cheek. "Can you get it for me?"

She nodded. "Yes, monsieur. It will take just a moment."

"Captain Renard and I will wait outside." He slipped out into the corridor. The German officer had gone downstairs with Piet, where, Jake knew, there would be a free drink waiting for him at the bar and his choice of any of Jake's other girls, free of charge. It was Jake's policy to provide satisfaction to all his customers, regardless of their needs or peccadilloes. This was something he had learned during his own tenure at Madame Fragonard's all those years ago in Paris.

Presently the door clicked open, and Lizbeth's face appeared. She passed Jake something wrapped in the handkerchief.

"This is it." He unwrapped it with trembling hands: a slender silver case, polished to a silken sheen.

"Very nice," Renard said dryly. "A cigar case."

"Oh no." It was hard to keep a note of smugness out of his voice, but Jake managed it, just barely. "Watch." He pulled at either end, and the silver case came apart, disgorging a sheaf of papers, folded and rolled so as to fit inside.

"What...." Renard peered at the documents Jake was holding. "Is that...?"

"The exit visas. Signed by General Weygand." Jake let out a breath, and then he was suddenly laughing.

"Yes, but...." Renard took the silver case from him and examined it. "Where did...?" It occurred to him with lightning swiftness, and he grinned. "Mon Dieu... that minx... that brilliant little minx!"

"No wonder she refused to service him." Jake shook his head. "She might as well have hung out a sign." He slid the documents into the inside pocket of his dinner jacket and tapped on Lizbeth's door. "Here you are," he said, handing back the case. "And thank you."

"Forgive me, Monsieur Jake. I did not mean to cause any disruption."

"You're a genius. Did Frederik tell you to take care of these for him?"

She nodded. "I am often a courier for Monsieur Abaroa."

Renard leaned back against the wall, one hand resting on his belt. "You know, Jake, my boy, I thought that I'd seen everything in my time. Simply ingenious." He glanced at his watch. "Have you got a safe place to keep those?"

"Yeah." Jake glanced around to make sure they hadn't been overheard. "Yeah, I'll put 'em somewhere safe."

Renard smirked. "Got a cigar case of your own?"

Jake slapped him on the back, pushing the policeman toward the stairs. "None of your damn business."

He could breathe again—for now, and perhaps only for a little while, but it was something.

It was something.


"Monsieur le capitaine, this is most irregular! I don't see how you can take responsibility for this, all on your own! What if something happens?"

"Oh, Andine, stop fussing. You're clucking like a hen." Renard pulled on his gloves. "Is my car ready?"

"Yes, monsieur. You want I should drive you?"

"No."

"But monsieur—"

"What I said, Andine, was no. If you have trouble understanding, might I suggest an ear specialist?"

Andine took a deep breath. "And if he kills you?"

"Don't be ridiculous. He isn't going to kill the chief of police in the middle of the souk. It's after curfew. A gunshot would be heard for miles."

"Monsieur, please... don't do this."

"Andine, mind the shop while I'm gone... and...." Renard wondered if there was anything else he should say. "There is a slight chance that I might not come back. Monsieur Jake might be annoyed. Will you give him my regrets?"

"Whatever monsieur le capitaine wishes," Andine said gloomily.

"*Très bien.*" Renard paused to tilt his hat at its usual rakish angle and was gone, his rapid steps vanishing quickly into the desert night.


Nicolas Renard killed the car's lights and rolled to a smooth stop some feet away from the souk's farthest stall. He sat very still, listening, but heard nothing beside the soughing of the desert winds and the lonely cry of some far-off night bird.

"Come out, come out, wherever you are." He smirked. "Talking to yourself, Renard. You really are getting old." He lit a cigarette, rolled down the window, and sat with all his senses straining into the darkness.

The souk was an unpleasant place after curfew, with its empty stalls and its general air of desolation. During the day, of course, it bustled with life, with sounds and voices, but now it had the look and feel of a cemetery. Renard shuddered and suppressed the urge to cross himself. He'd abandoned his religion a long time ago, and, anyway, he was starting at shadows. There was nothing here. Clearly his "contact" had been a ruse. He sat smoking until he nearly burned his fingers, and then threw the cigarette out the car window. He'd wait for half an hour, no more—if, as he suspected, no one showed up, then he'd leave. He was bone tired, and the pain in his face had reasserted itself, throbbing gently with each heartbeat. A nice cool bath and then bed… perhaps a little drink before he retired—just the one, no more.

The savagery of Yvette's murder bothered him more than he would readily admit to anyone. He'd seen a lot in his time, but the ferocious nature of this crime, the gaping wound in her throat, spoke of hatred and resentment. As far as Renard knew, she'd had no enemies in Maarif—at least none whose dislike of her would extend to outright murder—and the water, thrown over the corpse after the fact, bothered him. If her killer had wanted to wash her, he would have undressed her, or at least done a more thorough job. No, the water had been thrown over her, dashed in her face like—*Yes, well.* Renard grimaced. Some women of his acquaintance liked that sort of thing, but he failed to see the appeal of it. Love was supposed to be sensual, a heated congress of bodies and breath, of hands and mouths and skin—

*Dammit, Nicolas... don't... you're killing me with that... goddamn you....*

—not mutual degradation. Although he supposed it was possible that some people enjoyed it that way, just as some people chose to drink a lesser vintage. It had never made any sense to him, but then, much of what people did left him very puzzled.

*There.* Renard stiffened, his body suddenly rigid, his breath abruptly stilled. Just there, at the far edge of his vision, something or someone was moving toward him out of the darkness. The hair at the back of his neck prickled as the figure resolved and grew clearer. He fumbled with the door latch and felt the door swing away from him. He stepped out onto the sand, feeling as if he was moving in slow motion.

"I know what happened to that bitch." The figure was a young girl, perhaps twelve years old, stringy-haired and skinny, wearing a short flowered dress that hung on her like a sack, and not much else. "I know what cut her." She spoke French with a Toulon accent, and her voice was very low, almost masculine, and rough.

Renard allowed himself to relax. "Well, then, I should think you have a duty to report what you know." He indicated the big command car. "Would you like to sit down while I make out a report?"

"No." She backed away. "You don't report nothing. I'll tell you. That's all." She moved quickly, suddenly staring up at him. Her eyes seemed lit from within, the eyes of a madwoman. "You listen to what I have to tell you."

"Of course," Renard said. He held out a hand to her, but she didn't take it. "Not the friendly type, are you? Have you got a name?"

"My name's Mignon, or close enough. I knew Yvette. She came out here with that man, that German. She let him do things to her."

This was rubbish, Renard knew. Jake didn't allow his girls to operate outside the safe confines of Paradise. If a girl took on outside assignations, that was her business, but it was a business she could conduct without him. Any girl who tried it was immediately dismissed, and Renard knew Yvette wasn't that stupid.

"I very much doubt that. Now, have you got anything useful to tell me, or are you wasting my time?"

She spat on the ground, narrowly missing Renard's boot. "She's a whore."

"No," Renard said quietly, "she *was* a whore. Now she's dead."

The girl laughed soundlessly, showing a mouth full of rotting teeth. "That's why he blessed her. That's why Remy blessed her."

"Remy? Who is Remy?"

"Don't you know the Priest? That's what they call him. That's what everybody calls him." She advanced on him, jerking her chin in his direction. "He's coming to bless you now—didn't you know?"

Renard turned, a moment too late. The blade was already moving, coming down on him from the tallest man he had ever seen. He recognized the lantern jaw and the misshapen ears from police photos: Remy Said, a Bedouin who had turned against the traditional lifestyle of his people in favor of foraging in the city. He was well-known to Renard and his men and constituted little more than a public nuisance.

Renard instinctively threw his arms up to protect his head and face. The blade crunched into his shoulder with brutal, tearing force, and his left side was on fire. *You goddamn idiot.* He fumbled for his revolver and fired two shots before he fell down, down into blessed unconsciousness.


"But I don't understand. Where would he have gone? We were supposed to discuss things, he and I." If Christophe Picard had purposely set out to make a nuisance of himself, he could not have succeeded better than he was now doing. He had dogged Jake's heels from the moment he'd set foot in Paradise, and always the same refrain: Where was Nicolas Renard? "Jacob, I appeal to you… if you and I meant anything to each other—"

"Captain Renard and I aren't in the habit of checking in with each other." He contemplated the ledger in front of him while trying to ignore Picard. "He goes his way and I go mine. And if I were you, I wouldn't go bringing up any of that "Auld Lang Syne" stuff either. Bad for business." On the other side of the room, the band wailed "I'll Be Seeing You" while Piet deftly wove his way in and out of tables, carrying a laden tray. "You shouldn't even be in here, and I don't know what you're trying to prove in the first place." He fixed Picard with a look. "I stick my neck out for you after you show up here, and yet here you are, waltzing around like you own the place, like nobody would dare touch you in public."

Picard smirked. "They wouldn't."

"Don't be so sure of that, my friend. One of these days your luck might run out, and where would that pretty wife of yours be, then?"

"Ah. I wondered when we would get around to talking about Maartje."

"I wasn't talking about her." Jake lit a cigarette.

Picard sat at Jake's table. "Jake, please. What do I have to say to make you understand?"

"What's there to understand?" Jake's laughter was brittle. "I don't care who you're fucking." He flipped the ledger's pages violently. "Had to show her off, huh? Couldn't wait to rub my nose in it."

"It's not like that. That's not what this is at all."

"That's something I've been wondering." Jake took a long drag on the cigarette. "Just what is this? Oh, I know Danzig wants you. You escaped from Drancy, and so far you've spent the war prancing around Europe, thumbing your nose at him. Maybe they'll give him an Iron Cross when he captures you. I don't know and I sure as hell don't care." He flipped some pages, pretending to make notations as he went. His hands were shaking, and he was angrier than he'd been in a long time. "But there's a lot of people around here who believe in whatever it is you're doing."

"You used to believe in it, Jacob! There was a time when you and I believed the same things."

Jake laughed bitterly. "There was a time, my friend, when I worked in a whorehouse in the Rue Pigalle. Now I've got a place of my own. It's not much, but I like to think I've come up in the world."

Rolande smiled at Jake as she went past with what looked like two of Danzig's entourage. She was wearing a leather corset and black stockings, and she carried a whip and a gleam in her eye. The band was playing "I Don't Want to Set the World on Fire" as a skinny tenor with prominent ears stepped to the mike. Jake didn't remember hiring him, but that didn't necessarily worry him, as long as the kid could sing.

"You've done very well." Picard reached a hand across the table, not quite touching Jake's sleeve. "It is very important that I speak to Captain Renard. I am begging you, Jake."

"And I'm telling you I don't know where he is." Jake pushed away the ledger and took out a deck of cards. He began laying out a game of patience on the table, doing his best to ignore Picard. "Say, are you gonna spend any money in here? Because this is a whorehouse, and I can't really sit around chatting up the customers. It's bad for business."

Picard's smile was pained. "Would it help if I bought a bottle of champagne? Or do you still drink it by the glass?"

"No, Christophe, I don't drink it by the glass, and unlike my girls, I'm not for sale." He spied Guillaume Andine shouldering his way through the crowd and suppressed a groan. "Great. It seems I've got all the French after me tonight." He stood as Andine burst through a clutch of middle-aged Austrian women, all crouched around Piet, who had abandoned his tray and was telling an extremely long and complicated story that apparently had no end. "What do you want?"

"Monsieur Jake, you must come."

"No, I must not." Jake turned over a card. "Now see here, you boys have got to stop involving me in your troubles. What goes on in the rest of the world is none of my business."

"Monsieur Renard went out there."

Picard stiffened at Jake's side like a pointer. "Where?" he asked. "He went out where?"

"There was a message that came… it said someone had news about Yvette, and monsieur le capitaine had to go to the far end of the souk, after curfew."

The bottom of Jake's gut dropped like a stone. "Tell me he didn't go."

"*Bien sûr*, monsieur, he did go! I argued with him, but he wouldn't listen! You know how he is."

"Yeah," Jake said grimly, "I know how he is."

"He was supposed to meet an informant, someone who knew about Yvette." Andine raised his shoulders and let them drop. "He ought to have returned, but no, he is not here."

"How long has he been gone?"

"Two hours."

"Two *hours*?" Jake stared at him. "And you're only just telling me this now?" He grabbed Andine's shoulder and spun him around. "Come on. We're going. Piet!"

He came running. "What is it, Monsieur Jake?"

"Can you and Andy handle things? I've got an errand to run."

"Of course! I give them arak. I can hardly keep up with it! They drink and drink—we are the well at the end of the world!" He glanced at Andine and Picard. "These gentlemen, they are going with you as well, hmm?"

"They're going too." Jake went behind the bar, retrieved his revolver, and slipped it into his jacket. "Tell the band to keep it upbeat, okay? Too many slow songs are making everybody depressed."

"And where are you going with these gentlemen?" Piet hovered like an elderly aunt. "Or am I not permitted to know?"

"Captain Renard needs… a change of clothing."

The spotlight hovered, then swung around on the skinny tenor, who launched into "Poor Butterfly" with near-suicidal sadness.

Piet nodded, as if he heard this sort of thing every night of the week. "Of course! Police work, it is dirty." He glanced over his shoulder. "And what if Major Danzig should come in?"

Andine spat on the floor. *"Dis-lui d'aller se faire foutre."*

"None of that language in here." Jake poked Andine. "Come on. This needn't take all night."

"Andine said he'd gone to the souk," Picard said. "Where her body was found."

Jake shot him an annoyed look. "You seem to know an awful lot about this," he muttered.

Picard ignored the implied slur. "Perhaps one of your police vehicles?" he asked Andine. "Something fast. I believe time is of the essence in this case."


*WELL, THIS is just like Marseilles, and I am a bloody fool.* Nicolas Renard suspected much hadn't changed since his earlier years. He tried to keep his mind firmly fixed on that, but the pain in his shoulder was drilling through his consciousness. His arm hung limply at his side, blood dripping off his fingertips and pooling in the desert sand. He'd fired two shots, both impossibly wide, both missing the man and the girl. He knew the darkness and his injury had affected his aim. He knew, too, he'd been given a warning: the giant Remy, the killer who called himself the Priest, could have hacked him to bits and left him scattered in the desert. Or perhaps the sight of Renard's gun had scared him off.

*No.* Renard laughed at himself. *Listen to you, Nicolas, inventing excuses for your own shortcomings.* What happened to the brazen boy who kicked the backsides of the Boche all those years ago? Who had stumbled through the last big war with the American at his side, both of them scared spitless and terrified of dying before they had a chance to get laid.

*He's bleeding on the sand. He's probably going to die out here, and it serves him right for being such an idiot.*

Ah, well… everybody had to sometime, wasn't that correct? He'd hardly expect to live forever; he wasn't seventeen. Renard lay back on the sand and gazed up at the night sky. Really, the stars were beautiful in Maarif, and if one looked, one could make out the long arm of the galaxy, spiraling into the darkness of space, thousands upon thousands of sparkling nodes of light. It made a sort of train, the long end of a lady's scarf, delicate and perfumed.

He put his good hand to the ground and tried to push himself upright, but he wasn't strong enough. He lay back on the sand. The stars had moved. Had he been asleep? What was going on?

"You have to get up, monsieur." Yvette was bending over him, Yvette in her bows and ribbons, her long red hair streaming all around her. Such a beautiful girl. Such a very sweet girl. "Monsieur, you must get up." She knelt beside him in the sand. Surely, she must be a phantasm, a creation of his own tired brain. "You must keep pressure on the wound. Do you hear me? You must keep pressure…."

"KEEP PRESSURE on the wound!" Andine held Renard's torso while Christophe Picard lifted his legs into the car. "You must keep pressure on it." He folded a blanket and slipped it under Renard's head and covered him with another.

"He's bleeding a lot." Jake climbed into the back. "Where's the wound?" The left side of Renard's white uniform was soaked with dark blood that looked black in the moonlight. "He's bleeding all over the place. Why is he still bleeding?"

"Here." Picard took hold of Jake's hand and pressed it over Renard's upper arm. "Squeeze hard, as hard as you can."

"Something you learned in the concentration camp?" Jake asked.

Picard smiled. "You might say that." He adjusted the blanket under Renard's head, then glanced at Jake. "Are you all right? I can take your place, if—"

"It's fine." Jake bent over Renard. "Just get back as quick as you can. We'll have to go to the clinic. This isn't something you can wrap up with a handkerchief."

"How very clever you are, Jake." The voice was faint but unmistakably Renard's. He hissed through his teeth as the car jerked into motion. "Lieutenant Andine must be driving. That would explain the rough ride."

"Don't try to talk." Jake wondered if he looked as grim as he felt. "You'll be home soon."

"Oh, Jake." Renard reached out with his good hand and grasped a fold of Jake's sleeve. "You came after me. How delightfully mutual…." His head fell over to one side, and for a horrified moment, Jake thought he might be dead, but Renard's breathing, though ragged, was regular.

Jake didn't even look up to see their progress.

*Almost there. Hurry up.*

THE SMALL room in a nondescript little town in Oran was lit by a single bulb. The man within lay on his bed, listening to the radio, which at that moment was playing a jerky Arabic version of "I'm in the Mood for Love." There was a tap at the door, and he got up to answer it.

A young woman was there, her long black hair confined under a scarf. She was pale, with gray-green eyes and a sensuous mouth. He looked her over before taking out his wallet and laying a sheaf of francs on the bureau. The girl smiled. "That's a lot of money. How long has it been, monsieur?" Her voice was low and cultured, and she had a Marseillaise accent.

Frederik Abaroa swallowed and forced his attention away from his stiffening cock. "A long time, mademoiselle."

"Let me help you out of your clothes." She moved with the grace of a dancer as she reached for the buttons of his shirt. Abaroa forced himself to keep his hands at his sides, even though he ached to touch her. She smelled of roses and patchouli, and her hair brushed his face as she moved to undress him. She bent and flicked her tongue over the skin of his chest, dipping into the hollow of his throat and moving lower, circling each of his nipples. The muscles of his belly clenched as she dropped to her knees and reached for his fly. She pushed his trousers down and pressed her mouth against the front of his silk boxer shorts, breathing through the gossamer fabric, warming his flesh with her breath. She reached around his body and cupped his buttocks in her palms, squeezing him, kneading his flesh. His turgid cock strained against the thin silk, and she pulled the waistband of his shorts down, freeing him. "Such a lovely cock," she murmured. She took it in hand and rubbed the head gently over her lips, and as she traced the contours of her mouth, she flicked it with the very tip of her tongue. Abaroa whimpered and pushed against her mouth, and she chuckled. "A very long time, monsieur."

She led him to the bed and laid him down, and then she stripped off her blouse and released her full breasts from her bra. Abaroa groaned as she leaned over him and rubbed the generous, warm globes against his face. He caught her nipple in his mouth and pulled it in, sucking strongly. She cried out, "Oh, monsieur, you please me!" Abaroa clasped her waist in his strong hands and raised her over him, pulling her body tight against his. A long shudder ran through her when he clasped her rounded buttocks, and she sobbed aloud as Abaroa's long fingers closed around her swollen cock. "Monsieur, you find my secret." Her face was sad. "Now you will throw me out?"

"No." He kissed her, tongue delving into the hot, wet mouth as he quickly divested her of the thin skirt and satin panties. Her breasts rubbed his chest in an inviting manner, but it was the smooth, tawny globes of her perfect backside that intrigued him the most. He rubbed and squeezed them, pinched the skin and soothed the bright red marks. He parted the cheeks and teased her entrance with a finger. His desire was so strong that it threatened now to drown him, and his distended cock pulsed with every beat of his heart, his blood a primal throbbing in his head, his loins, and his belly. He whispered what he wished to do, and she nodded.

"There is oil in my purse. Let me fetch it for monsieur." She pressed the little vial into Abaroa's hand, explaining as she did so how it was to be used. "Only a little, monsieur. It is rare and precious, and it can burn the flesh." Abaroa spread a little on his fingers and reached to massage her entrance, circling around and around as she writhed and bucked and begged him for release. He pressed into her slowly, not wanting to cause her pain, gritting his teeth against a building tidal wave of pleasure that pounded at the base of his spine. He would come if she moved. She seemed to sense this and stayed perfectly still as he entered her fully.

Abaroa's body trembled, and he fought the urge to pound into her and end this delicious torment. He drew back slowly, hands on her hips, and the taut walls of her entrance tugged at him. He keened aloud, spoke some words in his native Basque, and pushed in again. She whimpered, and Abaroa reached around with one oil-slick hand to hold the girl's erection. Her cock slid against his greased palm in time with his thrusts. She writhed against him as Abaroa rode her, pounding into her harder and harder as his pleasure rose and blinded him, tearing his climax from him in three or four hard, blinding pulses that left him weak and voiceless. She reached for him and guided him again to her cock, and in three strokes, she was coming, spilling her seed over the sheets and Abaroa's hand. He slipped out of her and lay back on the bed, panting, eyes closed. He heard the sound of a cigarette lighter, and then a cigarette was slipped between his lips.

"What is your name?" she asked, and Abaroa told her. "I feel badly taking your money, monsieur. You have given me such pleasure." She kissed him, got up to dress, and tucked the sheaf of francs into her brassiere. "You would not like me to stay a little longer?"

Abaroa shook his head. "Thank you, no." He sighed. He would miss her wonderful ass, but they were at war and business was business. He held the door for her and locked it after she had gone. He had scarcely turned away when someone knocked. "Yes?"

"The ants are marching," a voice said.

A piece of paper was shoved through the door at him. He took it and read it. "Tonight?"

"*Bien sûr*," the voice said. "As soon as possible."

THE NIGHT was hot, and the heat lay over the tiny Oran train station like a shroud. Frederik Abaroa, sweating inside his linen suit, paced the platform smoking a cigarette. The train, which should have arrived an hour ago, was taking a notoriously long time, and it made him nervous. He was running on a tight schedule and needed to be back in Maarif—not standing on a rickety platform in the middle of the night, smoking himself into a state of nervous exhaustion. His body still hurt from the damage inflicted on it by Danzig's goons, but that was nothing compared to the outrage he felt at the most recent news. His contact was good—one of the very best, in fact, hand-picked by Christophe Picard—and if Abaroa trusted no one else in Maarif, he trusted Picard. Picard was one of two men who, despite his personal transgressions, always impressed Abaroa as essentially honorable. The other was Nicolas Renard, a sentiment that, should it ever have been heard by anyone, would cause howls of laughter from Maarif to the Horn of Africa.

There were a lot of soldiers at the station, and even more of them on Abaroa's train. At each stop, several uniformed men got on, most of them in full battledress, soldiers of all nations. There were legionnaires in their white *kepi*s, chatting quietly in French and smoking, a Scotsman in the uniform of the Parachute Regiment, and four Americans arguing about baseball scores. A group of Canadians got on, all of them carrying full packs and extra ammunition. Abaroa listened to their plethora of accents with fascination.

A fat man in a brown suit sat beside Abaroa, sweating heavily. "Damned hot in this train, sir." He took out a handkerchief, mopped his face, and wiped inside the brim of his brown bowler hat. "Damned hot, I say."

Abaroa, amused, tried not to be. "North Africa is like that, sir."

"Don't see why it has to be so, sir." The fat man carried a rattan cane, which he laid on the floor of the carriage, and a deck of playing cards. "Don't see why it has to be so. Why, the power of the mind can change a great many things, sir! Yes, indeed." He shuffled the cards in his fat hands, grunting and talking to himself. What Abaroa initially took to be playing cards were actually photographs. He turned up a picture of a tall, gangly man with big ears and a lantern jaw—a candidate for the diagnosis of gigantism if Abaroa ever saw one. "Look at that! The face of an ugly dog, sir."

"A face only a mother could love," Abaroa remarked.

"Or a priest, sir." The fat man shuffled the cards and put them away. "Or a priest."

Abaroa wondered what Renard would say when he appeared back in Maarif, and he decided he didn't really want to know. It had taken considerable effort and expense to get Abaroa out of Danzig's clutches in the first place, and Renard would probably have a fit when Abaroa showed up, right back where he was least expected to be. But it couldn't be helped. If the intelligence was correct—and Abaroa had no reason to suspect otherwise—then Renard had somehow been compromised, and the lives of Christophe and Maartje Picard were in serious danger. He wasn't naïve and knew getting someone like Picard out of Maarif was going to be a difficult undertaking. He also wasn't ready to see that undertaking fail just because Danzig had come up with some new way to intercept the efforts of the Resistance.

Abaroa laid his forehead against the window glass. *I won't sleep. I won't.* Some part of him wanted to be awake when the train rolled into Maarif, but the hypnotic sound of the steel wheels was too much. He slipped into dreams as into a warm sea—he was suddenly back in Algiers, walking the dusty streets as he had done in years before. The wind was blowing hard, and he was cold, and the rags he wore were insufficient for the weather. He stumbled, and looking down, he noticed his feet were bleeding. He sat in a doorway and laid his head in his hands. *Now Christophe will come*, the waking part of his mind thought. *Christophe will reach out and lift me up*.... A hand appeared at the edge of his vision, and he reached for it, allowed himself to be pulled to his feet. He raised his eyes, expecting to see Christophe Picard, but saw Nicolas Renard instead.


THE NURSING sister was very tall, very beautiful, and extremely capable—a dark young woman with huge, liquid eyes. She was doing her best to keep Jake at bay while the doctors tended to the wound in Renard's shoulder.

Jake paced, smoking a succession of cigarettes while Picard sat slumped by the door, as if he'd been dropped into his chair from a height. What was going through Picard's mind was anybody's guess: he was probably thinking about how he and Maartje were going to get out of Maarif with their skins intact, now that Renard had been taken out of action. Picard was a creature of inscrutable mien, a man used to burying his emotions under a cloak of indifference. He was someone, Jake reflected, who could turn his feelings off and on like a light. Such extreme emotional malleability would have served him well in a concentration camp. Picard could be as warm and loving as the next man when it suited him—and in the next minute, turn cold and calculating, absolutely nasty, without so much as a whisper of warning.

"Haven't they finished yet?" Jake went to where the nursing sister stood, folding some clean towels. "How long's it take to stitch him up? Or is there something you aren't telling me?"

"Monsieur Plenty, please. If you would just sit down—"

A car pulled up just outside the front door, there was the sound of running footsteps, and then Maartje burst into the room. She had eyes only for her husband. "Christophe, I thought—" She stared, horrified, at the bloom of dark blood on his clothes.

The sister slipped into Renard's room and closed the door behind her.

"It isn't mine." He embraced her briefly. "Captain Renard—"

"Is he…?"

"Yeah, Captain Renard's been stabbed," Jake said. He drew on his cigarette and regarded her through narrowed eyes. "But he's all right. You can go home now." His tone skated a very thin line between abrupt and rude. "Nothing to see here."

Maartje started toward him. "Mr. Plenty, I wonder if—"

He pulled back from her reach. "You probably shouldn't touch me. You might get blood on your dress. We wouldn't want that."

The temperature in the room seemed to drop by a dozen degrees. Maartje stepped back and nodded, once. She seemed to know instinctively that there was history between Jake Plenty and

Christophe Picard, but not what kind. Maybe Jake would take it upon himself to enlighten the girl. Yeah, maybe he'd do that.

"Mr. Plenty." The sister appeared. "You may come in if you wish." She nodded at Christophe Picard and Maartje. "You may visit with your friend as well, but please, no more than five minutes."

Renard was awake but sedated and clearly still in a great deal of pain. A thick bandage encased most of his shoulder and arm. Jake surged toward him, struggling to contain his emotions.

"Now, then, Jake, there's no need for the long face." Renard reached out with his good hand, and Jake grasped it, held on to it like a lifeline, and Christophe Picard suddenly understood why Jake was so angry.

*It isn't me*, he thought, *not anymore*. He wondered if he were jealous. Jake's longing to touch Renard—to embrace him—was so evident, it was almost another presence in the room.

"Are you trying to get killed, is that it?" Jake's thumb stroked the back of Renard's hand, moving in small circles. He seemed unaware he was even doing it. "Trying to get sympathy? Andine told us what you did, going out there all by yourself."

"Perhaps Monsieur Jake might like to reserve this particular discussion for another time." The nursing sister had come back into the room with a jug of water.

"She's a lioness, Jake." Renard smiled sleepily. "Better behave yourself." He smiled at the girl as she slipped quietly out of the room.

Renard noticed Maartje standing with Picard by the door. "Monsieur Picard acquitted himself quite well during my little incident, madame. I should think he were used to this sort of thing… and I must apologize. One ought never to receive a lady in such a state of undress."

"You need not worry about that. I'm happy that you are all right." Maartje leaned down to kiss his cheek. "Get well very soon."

"Of course," Jake said. "You both need him to get out of Maarif, isn't that right?"

Picard bristled. "Don't be like that, Jacob."

A muscle twitched in Jake's jaw and the thumb stroking circles on Renard's hand stilled for a moment. "I think the young lady out there said five minutes."

Maartje's mouth tightened. "Come on, Christophe." The door clicked shut behind them.

"Jake," Renard chided him, "you could have been nicer to them."

"Old news." He gripped Renard's hand with both of his. "Nicolas, when you get out of here, we're going to have a serious talk, me and you."

Renard struggled to focus on him. "Are we?"

"Yes, we are. About following dubious intelligence into the desert, and going off to get yourself stabbed and almost killed."

"Do you know how beautiful you are when you're angry?" Renard's pulse beat steadily at the base of his throat, and Jake quashed an urge to lean in and kiss him there, breathe in the scent of him.

"Don't start that."

"Getting coy in your old… old age?" Renard's eyelids slid shut. "Almost… as coy as me."

Jake sat watching him for a few moments, reassuring himself that the rise and fall of Renard's chest was regular. He felt about a thousand years old—how long had it been since Andine had turned up with the news that Renard was overdue? He dropped his head and rubbed his eyelids with his free hand. His eyes felt like there were grains of sand embedded under the lids. He'd left Andy and Piet in charge of the club, but they would have long since closed up by now. Jake sighed, trying to put it out of his mind.

Nicolas was right: he had been rude to Maartje. But dammit, it couldn't just be water under the bridge to him, not now and not ever. He wasn't sure how much Christophe had told her, or if he'd even told her anything at all, and Jake didn't really care. It wasn't his job to protect Picard's reputation—what was left of it—and whatever loyalty he might have felt for Picard had gone the way of the dodo. What Picard had done to him had left him bitter and cynical and used up. Impossible that he should ever love anyone the way he….

Anyway.

The sister had said five minutes, and Jake was certain he'd long since overstayed his welcome. He eased his fingers out of Renard's grip.

"No." Renard's voice was husky, heavy with sleep. "Don't go. I want you to stay."

Jake bent close and stroked his cheek. "They won't let me."

"Tell them you're in love with me." Renard grinned. "You are in love with me, aren't you, Jake?"

"Nicolas, why'd you let Danzig do that to you?"

"That's supposed to be a secret." Renard opened sleepy eyes, but only for a moment. "He wasn't supposed to tell you. I asked him not to tell you...." He fell profoundly asleep, the medication finally overcoming his will.

"Nicolas." Jake uncurled the fingers of Renard's good hand and kissed the palm. "You goddamned idiot." He jerked away as the door swung open.

The nursing sister appeared, filling the doorway like a vision. "It's time, Monsieur Plenty. I am sorry." She leaned over Renard and adjusted the bedcovers. "He will sleep through the night." She smiled. "I suggest you try to do the same thing."

Jake nodded. "Can you contact me if he wakes up? He might need—" He caught himself. "—something."

"I will do as you ask. Now go home and get some rest. He will be awake for you in the morning."

# CHAPTER
# EIGHT

FREDERIK ABAROA was awake when the train pulled into Maarif—awake and grateful it was night. He pulled himself upright in his seat and scrubbed sleep out of his eyes with his taped, painful fingers. Ah yes, back in Maarif, alone in the dark, and waiting to see which way the wheel of Fate would spin. Such a joy it was, this war. Someday he would look back on it and laugh—if he survived.

He waited till the rest of the passengers had disembarked before taking his valise and stepping onto the platform. He scanned the station and its surroundings, but the place was better than empty, with only one sleepy-looking gendarme on duty by the little stand that sold newspapers and cigarettes. Abaroa bought himself a packet of Gauloises and a copy of the local paper. He found a taxi waiting underneath a lamppost and got in.

Emil was waiting for him. "I'm sorry we had to bring you back this way. I understand you have no love for Maarif and no wish to be back here." He leaned forward and tapped the driver—a huge, portly man with a partly bald head—on the shoulder. The taxi pulled onto the main street, headed for the center of Maarif.

"How is he?" Abaroa rested his bandaged hands on his knees and gazed down at them. The doctor in Oran said the breaks had begun healing nicely. As long as the fingers weren't broken again, everything would be fine. Abaroa wondered what bones Danzig's goons would break this time when they found him. It wasn't a pleasant thought.

"He was taken to the clinic. Monsieur Jake said he is resting comfortably. It was only a flesh wound, and the doctors have stitched it up."

"He is a good man."

"Yes."

They rode in silence for some time through streets that were empty and dark. Now and then the searchlight would sweep across the town, briefly illuminating their faces: Emil's, tense and pale, and Abaroa's, resigned and empty. At length the car pulled up in front of Jake's Paradise, and Emil leaned forward and gave the driver a handful of francs. The quick glimpse that Abaroa had was of a round, genial, fat face and small, smiling eyes. If the light had been better, he should have sworn that driver was Hassan Abbass, owner of the tea shop by the souk.

Emil held the door open, and they slipped inside—it wouldn't do to be seen. Emil led Abaroa through the silent club and up the stairs to Jake's apartment, where he knocked and waited.

"Yeah."

"Mr. Abaroa is here."

The door swung open, and Jake stood there, disheveled and exhausted, holding a glass of whiskey. "Come on in, Frederik. Emil, thanks a million." He waited till Emil had gone, then showed Abaroa to a chair and poured him a drink. "You didn't have to come back."

"Yes," Abaroa said, "I did." He sipped his whiskey, grateful for its slow burn. "You see, the entire process is in danger of falling off the rails." He regarded Jake for a moment as he lit a cigarette. "Do you think Danzig was behind what happened to Yvette?"

"Hard to say. Maybe he finds himself in the same position as a certain Dr. Frankenstein. God knows, anybody can find a crazy to hire around here. You don't have to walk far." Jake felt in his pockets for his own cigarettes, finally gave up, and accepted a cigarette from Abaroa. "He wasn't satisfied with what he did to you, what he did to Nicolas—I mean, what he personally did to Nicolas."

Abaroa was nonplussed. "What… what did he do to Nicolas?"

"You mean, you don't know?" Jake told him.

Abaroa cursed fluently and at some length. "He was bleeding… that night at his house, I remember it… he came out of the bathroom and there was…." *A pool of blood underneath his heel.* "He told me it was nothing, that his houseboy Ali would tend to it." Abaroa pressed his fists into his eyes. "Danzig probably had Yvette murdered just to draw Nicolas in. That's got Gestapo written all over it. Has anyone told Ali?"

"Wait," Jake said. "I'll go out there later. I'm sure Ali is used to Captain Renard coming home late or sometimes not at all. No sense in alarming him if we don't have to. He'll be fine. Major Danzig, however, isn't going to be fine when all this is over. I'm going to find whoever did this to Captain Renard. I'm going to trace this filthy river right back to its source."

"Jake, I think what you need is to sleep." Abaroa stood. "You look like—"

"Yeah, I guess I do. You okay with the guest room?"

Abaroa nodded. "I can sleep anywhere."

"Want something to eat?"

"No." He shuddered as though someone were walking over his grave. "I just want this over with."


NICOLAS RENARD was dozing lightly when something got between him and the lamp at his bedside. "What do you want?" It seemed perfectly natural to him that a man in full Nazi uniform should appear before him now, standing in the spotless hospital room, his whole being possessed with an aura of waiting.

"Captain Renard, I think it is very important that we have a talk." Aleksander Danzig pulled a chair to the side of the bed and sat.

Fishing a cigarette case out of his breast pocket, he lit one and puffed on it contentedly. "You do not mind if I smoke?"

"Oh, not at all." Renard was careful not to let his alarm show on his face. He knew Danzig went armed—knew, too, that Danzig was a sadistic bastard who'd like nothing better than to pump the hospital staff—and Renard—full of lead.

"Captain Renard, some things have been happening lately in Maarif that you will agree are troublesome. The murder of this… woman is, of course, unfortunate, but what else can one expect? It is Feldwebel Stussel I am most concerned about and, of course, you. You realize that you are placing yourself in great danger—"

"Why exactly did you have Yvette killed? Why hire a Bedouin assassin to do it? That's like taking a sledgehammer to kill a fly." Renard reached for his own cigarettes and lit one. "I've been lying here mulling that over, Danzig, and I can't for the life of me figure it out. So Stussel was with her when he was killed. It's highly unlikely that she killed him… and not very good for business. Why would you want to get her out of the way? She was no threat to you."

A muscle near Danzig's mouth twitched and he smiled thinly. "I am a representative of the Reich, captain, wherever I go."

"So you were cleaning house? Is that it?" Renard snorted. "Sorry, I'm not buying it." He tapped ash off his cigarette. "No, my bet is that Stussel told Yvette something he shouldn't have, and you were terrified she'd tell someone else, so you made sure that wouldn't happen." He smiled. "What did Yvette know, major? What was Stussel carrying that was so important—that you *missed*?"

Danzig's eyes narrowed, leaned over, and slapped Renard hard in the face. "You place yourself in great peril, captain." Danzig was breathing hard, fighting to control his emotions, which were in danger of taking him over completely. "We have a complete dossier on you, as well as your friend Mr. Plenty. We are aware of your unusual interests. The Third Reich will not countenance such men as you." Danzig moved his chair closer to the bed and laid his arm on Renard's chest, pressing down and causing great pain. "Do you know what waits for you, captain? A concentration camp. A concentration camp, captain, and a pink triangle to sew on your uniform. If you are very, very lucky, you will drop dead of hunger and exhaustion before we find it necessary to experiment on you." He removed his arm from Renard's chest and sat back. Renard was gray-faced and breathing heavily. "Our scientists are most interested in finding out what makes a degenerate. I, for one, would appreciate watching them dissect *your* brain, captain."

"So, you don't know either." Renard fought to keep his voice steady, to not betray the fear coursing through his veins on an adrenaline tide. Danzig could kill him—extinguish him before Renard had time to warn the others—and his men would exterminate the rest of them, Christophe Picard and Maartje and Abaroa and Jake, and there was nothing, *nothing* Renard could do to stop him. "You've no idea what Stussel was carrying." Renard clenched his fists to keep his hands from shaking. "Just like that day at the airport when I asked you about it. You'd no idea then either. All of this is going on around you, and you haven't got one single goddamn clue...."

Danzig's fist smashed into Renard's face, a savage blow that bounced his head off the iron bed frame. The darkness closed in, and Renard was unconscious.

Danzig turned on one elegantly booted heel and left the hospital room.


It WAS a night like any other at Jake's Paradise: the tenor was at the mike singing "It Had to Be You" while rapt patrons sat listening, sipping their champagne cocktails, and making their assignations. Jake, freshly shaved and dressed in a tuxedo and black tie, was moving slowly through the crowd, watching. He always watched, even when he didn't seem to be looking at anything in particular. His attention swept the room like the ever-present German searchlight that followed all their nocturnal comings and goings—to the casual observer, he was just another brothel keeper presiding over his personal domain. Those who worked for him knew better. Andy, bustling in and out of the kitchen with laden trays, was sweating more than was usual in

Maarif's humid heat, and Piet kept sneaking looks over his shoulder at the door, as if expecting someone. They had all been briefed by Jake, long before Paradise opened for the evening, and everybody knew it was more than his life was worth to breathe a word about what was upstairs in Jake's extra bedroom.

Frederik Abaroa lay on Jake's spare bed, trying to read a newspaper. Abaroa was as nervous as anyone in Paradise below, even though he knew nerves were of little use in this situation. Abaroa wasn't a jittery man as a rule. He'd been in the service of the Resistance since the war began, and long before that he had trained alongside Christophe Picard, learning the fine art of covert forays into enemy territory. He trusted Jake insofar as he trusted anyone, but Jake was only a man, and, Abaroa knew, men made mistakes. It wasn't that Jake wasn't brave, but Abaroa knew from looking at him that Jake had very recently suffered a violent blow to the heart. This emotional wound had peeled away some of his carefully tendered reserve. What Aleksander Danzig had done to Nicolas Renard was repugnant in the extreme and violated every convention of modern warfare. Jake loved Renard, even if he couldn't yet admit it to himself—that was plain enough to anyone who had eyes to see, and Frederik Abaroa noticed more than most people. The cynical American with the hard-bitten heart had finally been touched in the place he least expected, in a way he least expected.

As for Danzig…. Abaroa snorted to himself through a mouthful of cigarette smoke. He deserved whatever he got, and Abaroa fervently hoped Jake would get the pleasure of tearing Danzig to pieces in the way that satisfied him best. Abaroa hoped he'd be around to see it, and maybe, if he was very lucky, Jake might let him have a poke or two himself.

"MY DARLING girl, I understand your concerns, but really, if I have to stay in this bed one more minute, I will lose my mind." Renard sat on the edge of his hospital bed, fully clad from the waist down and trying unsuccessfully to shrug into his shirt. "Be a good girl and help me into this, would you?"

"Monsieur le capitaine should not be out of bed. The doctor said—"

"Yes, the doctor." Renard sighed. It wasn't her fault; she was merely doing her job. "Manon, my darling." He patted the bed and she sat beside him. "Do you know, you are beautiful and clever and terribly good at what you do." How to explain to her—to anyone— that something much larger and more important required intervention, and it would not do to loiter. He suddenly remembered a scene from many years before: standing with his father at the wharf in Calais, one hand on the railing of the gangplank.

*Nicolas, you must go aboard now. Quickly, there is no time!*

His father had died while Renard was a legionnaire. A letter came one day from Toulon, the envelope smudged with myriad fingerprints and bearing a postmark three months in the past. Renard read it in the trenches of Gallipoli and stowed it in his tunic. The next day, his battalion was shelled, and he waited out the rest of the war in a Scottish hospital. He had even lost track of Jake, who was captured by Turks, taken into custody, and made to wait for rescue or the war's end.

*Why'd you do it, Nick? Why'd you come after me?* Years later, sitting outside of Paradise and drinking cognac from elegant little cups—*How Moroccan,* Renard thought. *A sign that he and Jake had both assimilated themselves to desert life.*—and watching the searchlight trace its endless track across the night sky. *Why'd you come and get me?*

What sort of answer could he possibly give? *Because I love you. Because I have always loved you. Because I loved you from the first day I ever saw you sitting with your back against a wall, sunning yourself on Corsica. Because I lie awake at night and think about you, because I ache for you, because I would ask your hand in marriage if I could.*

No—he had never said any of those things. When it came down to it, he hadn't the courage to lay his heart bare before his best friend, and so he'd offered some convenient fiction: *No man left behind, Jake. You know that.*

"Monsieur le Capitaine is well known in Maarif. It is said that Monsieur le Capitaine Renard is a charmer." She stilled his wandering hand, where it was trying to creep up her thigh.

"Do you think I am charming, Manon? Do you care for me at all?" He seized her hand and kissed the palm. It was important to maintain appearances, after all. "Then you must understand that, as much as I adore you, I really must be going."

"It is late at night. Monsieur le Capitaine ought to wait till the morning at least."

"Manon…." He hovered near her, gazing deep into her eyes. "*Ma chérie*, Manon…." He lifted a stray strand of hair off her face. "You are so very, very lovely…."

"Where is le capitaine going?"

"Le capitaine has work to do. A woman has been murdered." He lingered close to her, his mouth inches from hers. "Don't you think I should help to bring her killer to justice?" Renard dropped his eyes, his gaze following the luscious curve of her full breasts. He was giving her the fullest benefit of his considerable experience. Normally the girl would have been swooning by now, but Renard's heart, he had to admit, wasn't in it. Whenever he gazed at Manon, lovely Manon, he saw a brooding, cynical face and a pair of deep, sad eyes. Whenever he leaned close to her voluptuous charms, he longed to be crushed against a hard, muscled chest and held in Jake Plenty's arms. He sighed. This wasn't working. "My darling girl. I really am sorry, but I have been away from duty long enough."

"They say you are a great connoisseur of women." She was suddenly shy with him, and twin spots of warm color burned high up on her cheekbones. "That you love women as other men love wine. They say that your bed is never empty." She held his shirt for him. "Is that true?"

"Do you know, Manon… it was true. Until very recently." He grimaced as the shirt slid over his sore shoulder.

"What happened?"

"I… I fell in love."

"Oh." She raised her eyebrows.

"Mmm. Let's keep that between us, shall we?" Renard stood up, slid into his jacket, and Manon helped him to fasten his Sam Browne.

She located his hat and handed it to him. "Are you certain you are well enough?"

"Lieutenant Andine is waiting for me in the car. I am well enough." He pressed her hand. "Thank you for everything you have done. You really are an angel of mercy."

"Mmmm," she said, "because I let you go?"

Renard set his hat on his head and tipped it at its usually jaunty angle. "That's part of the reason." He sketched a quick bow and left, eager to get the smell of antiseptics out of his nostrils.

Andine was sitting in the car just outside the clinic, and, seeing Renard, he hopped out and opened the door. "Monsieur, you look well. We were extremely worried. I myself was worried the most, although some of the others were worried as well. Myself, I think you should not have gone out into the desert by yourself—"

"Andine, do stop. I have a flesh wound to my shoulder. It's hardly a death warrant."

"Yes, monsieur." Andine was pleased to see his superior, however, and the smile kept creeping back to his face. "Where should monsieur like to go?"

"Take me to Paradise. I need to talk to Jake immediately."

"But…." Andine was puzzled. "You saw Monsieur Jake this morning. He went to visit you."

Renard stared at him. "You know, Andine, had your relatives not slept their way to the top of the préfecture de police, I'm not sure where you would be now. Making coffee, perhaps."

Andine pretended to be hurt. "Monsieur, there is no need to be nasty."

"What I have to say to Jake Plenty is business. Do you hear me? Official police business." The streets were empty at this hour, which was as it should be. Danzig would want to keep an eye on Jake and Renard, so he and his men would most likely be in Paradise, with any luck at all. Hopefully Jake had convinced Christophe Picard to stay out of sight, although if necessary, Renard would arrest him and his pretty wife too and keep them in custody until they could be shoved aboard the next convenient Portugal-bound plane.

"He looks very good in that tuxedo, does Monsieur Jake." Andine wasn't quite smirking.

"I beg your pardon?" They were passing by the souk now, where he had found Yvette's body and where the strange Bedouin calling himself the Priest had inflicted Renard's wound. Probably Danzig had chosen him especially, thinking Renard was the sort to jump at bogeymen. He might as well have sent Boris Karloff to do the job instead. God forbid Danzig get his hands dirty. His kind were all for giving the orders, as long as they weren't required to carry out the nasty business personally.

Andine tilted a glance at him. "I have an appreciation of fine clothes."

"Yes. Other men's clothes." Renard gazed through the windscreen as they turned onto the main street of Maarif. "You can drop me at Paradise. I'll meet you back at headquarters."

"I am not certain that is wise, monsieur. If something were to happen...."

"Nothing is going to happen."

Jake had held his hand... in the hospital, Jake had sat beside his bed and held his hand, and, of course, it merely looked like the action of a comrade and a friend.... *Tell them you're in love with me.* That was something Renard couldn't figure out: he and Jake had known each other for years, so why had it taken Jake so long to make overtures? Why had he waited years to touch Renard as he must have known Renard yearned to be touched? Why now? It wasn't until Renard had mentioned Salazar was coming to Maarif—that was when Jake had suddenly made a play for Renard, and, examined in that light, it made perfect sense that Jake would want to... use Renard to make Christophe Picard jealous. It was an unsettling thought.

The car stopped in front of Paradise. "Perhaps I should accompany you, monsieur, in case there is trouble?"

"Andine...." Renard awkwardly reached for the door handle. The pain in his shoulder had reasserted itself, burning along the nerve pathways in his neck. "Take the car around back." He sighed. "Perhaps you are right. It wouldn't hurt to have you nearby in case I need you."

"Monsieur le capitaine is very wise."

"Don't toady, Andine. You're not very good at it."

THE BAND was going great guns when Emil slipped inside to find Jake standing by the bar. "Monsieur Jake, you have a visitor."

"A visitor?" Jake glanced around but saw no one he knew in the crowd. "What's he look like?"

"A tall man, thin, with green eyes. He said he would wait in your apartment."

"You let some guy into my room? What the hell have I told you?" Jake crushed out his cigarette and, taking Emil by the elbow, steered him toward the stairs. "I should fire you on the spot! Are you out of your mind?"

"He said he was a personal friend of yours, Monsieur Jake. I meant no harm."

"Goddamn idiot." This was bad—this was very, very bad. Jake hated surprises, and more than that, he hated unexpected visits from people calling themselves his personal friends. Emil was getting sloppy. This was the sort of mistake he'd expect from one of the new guys, not somebody like Emil, who had been with Jake since he first came to Maarif.

"I am very sorry, monsieur." Emil pushed open the door and waited while Jake examined the interior. "It shall not happen again."

Jake's lips tightened. He was much angrier than he was letting on. "Get out of here. I'll deal with you later."

Chastened and ashamed, Emil vanished down the stairs.

Jake checked the windows and the rear door, and gave the dial on the safe an extra turn for good luck. He replenished his cigarette case from the box on his desk. "Who's there?"

Something had moved in the shadows, something tall and pale and draped in white. "Jacob. Don't be angry with me."

*Jesus Christ.* "Christophe!" Jake took a deep breath. "You losing your mind? Danzig's men are all over the place!"

"I came up the back way. Emil let me in. He said he recognized me from the newspapers." Picard's pale eyes were shining with an unnatural brightness, a martyr's confidence. "I had to see you before I go. This may be the last time, Jacob. Once I leave Maarif…."

"You shouldn't be here, not now. It's too dangerous." He moved to take Picard's arm. "I want you to go back to the hotel and wait with Maartje until—"

"No, Jacob, please." Picard pulled against him, resisting. "I had to see you." Tears trembled on his dark lashes, and he was shivering like a wild animal in a trap. Jake couldn't shake the feeling that all this was a performance crafted especially for his benefit. "Once I go, you and I will probably never see each other again. I couldn't leave Maarif without trying to explain about what happened between us in Paris."

Jake's expression hardened. "Paris is in the past. Go back to your wife and wait until I come to take you to the airport."

"Jacob, please." Picard took Jake into his arms and held him, their bodies pressed together, and in an instant, it all came back: Paris, the long, lazy afternoons in Madame Fragonard's, evenings spent making love in Jake's bedroom. *Do you know what I want, Jacob? I would like to pleasure you.*

*Of course, monsieur. That's why I'm here, after all.*

"This doesn't matter." *And I don't have time for this right now.* "It's not important." He tried to tell himself it meant nothing, that his body wasn't responding to Picard the way it always had, yet there was still some part of him that wanted to drive Picard back against the wall and kiss him until they melted together like they used to do, all heated hands and aching mouths.

"Please, just kiss me. Just kiss me, Jacob. This will be the last time for us, you know it." He cupped Jake's face in his hands and pressed his open mouth against Jake's. The sound of the band seemed to fade, and the familiar contours of Jake's apartment disappeared into a roaring tumult of memory. Jake clutched at Picard, held him tight, plundering his mouth as if he meant it, which some part of him did, and always would.


"Monsieur Renard! So good to see you again!" Piet came hurrying up to him and tutted over the sling Renard wore. "Maarif is no longer safe in the nighttime! Things are getting worse."

"Maarif has never been safe in the night or any other time, Piet." Renard smiled. "Is Jake about the premises?"

"Mr. Jake is upstairs. He went up to check something for Emil. I think he is still up there."

"Thank you. I'll go on up if I may."

"He will be glad to see that you are out of the hospital, monsieur." Someone at one of the outlying tables called for a waiter, and Piet hurried off.

Renard started up the stairs, stopped on the landing, and pushed on Jake's partially opened door. "Jake, are you hiding from—"

Christophe Picard… and Jake. Christophe Picard and Jake, kissing. The strobing searchlight passed over their faces, illuminating all too clearly the hunger with which they caressed each other, and Renard felt as if he'd fallen through a hole in the earth.

For several long moments, he stood as if rooted, staring at them as a slow flush burned up his neck and into his face. "I beg your pardon." He turned on his heel, heard Picard's gasp and Jake's muttered curse, and then he was down the stairs and through the club and out into the night. He couldn't breathe. It felt like someone was sitting on his chest. He leaned against the wall, forcing air into his lungs in great, whooping breaths, and this was how Andine found him.

"Monsieur Renard! What is the matter?"

"Nothing's the matter." Jake's voice, taut as a wire. "Nicolas, come in here."

Renard straightened up. "No, Jake, I don't believe I will. I've seen as much of the floor show tonight as I can manage, thank you all the same."

Andine stared at Renard and Jake, confused. "I don't understand… floor show?"

"It's okay, lieutenant. You can go on inside. Captain Renard and I can talk out here." He held on to Renard's good arm and waited till Andine had gone. "Nicolas."

"Jake. Or perhaps I should call you Jacob. That's what he calls you, isn't it?"

"Come over here and sit down."

"No, I don't believe I will."

"Nicolas, please." Jake's grasp tightened on his arm. "Please."

He let himself be guided to one of the small tables set just outside the brothel's front door. The ever-present searchlight stroked the velvet sky, swinging around again. Renard was the first to speak. "You know, Jake, I'm a fool. I should have known." He plucked an invisible speck of dust from the leg of his uniform trousers. "I should have known that one night's sport hardly makes a… romance. Or even a fling." He gazed at Jake, sitting across the table from him, mute and miserable. "But you and Monsieur Picard—Salazar—you've got nostalgia. And I may not be the smartest man in Maarif, but I know I can't compete with that. I can't compete with a ghost, even the ghost of an old romance." He stood to go, sick at heart.

"Nicolas."

"Yes, you've said that already."

"We're in public."

"How very perceptive."

"What I mean is…." Jake moved closer. "If we weren't in public, I'd take you in my arms and kiss you like there's no tomorrow. But this is Morocco and I can't do that, Nicolas, even if it's what you and I both want."

"But you can sneak up to your apartment and kiss him." It sounded petty, juvenile, and jealous, and he was ashamed of himself. "I'm supposed to be a man of the world, Jake. Worse than that, I'm French, which means I'm supposed to take this in stride and laugh it off. Isn't that what sophisticated people do?"

Jake grasped his arm and pulled Renard as close as he dared. "I don't give a damn what sophisticated people do because I'm not in love with him. I'm in love with you."

It rang between them, that declaration, like resonating hammer blows. They stared at each other, chests rising and falling, breaths almost in unison. "So." Renard wasn't about to be mollified. "You kiss him because you're in love with me?"

"No, I kissed him because sometimes—dammit, Nicolas!—sometimes old ghosts come sliding up the stairs and beg you for something to take away with them before they leave for good. And that's all it was."

*You're a very poor liar*, Renard thought.

"And soon enough they leave Maarif on the plane to Lisbon."

Renard tilted his head. "So he gets to break your heart all over again. How sad. Poor Jake. You'll excuse me, of course, if I decline to take part. I may be French, but I have never had a taste for farce. *Bonsoir,* Jake." He turned on his heel and walked away.

Jake cursed softly and went inside. Guillaume Andine was standing by the bar, looking distinctly uncomfortable.

"Monsieur Jake, I realize it is none of my business…."

"You're right." Jake struck a match off the edge of the bar and lit a cigarette. "It isn't, but that never seems to stop you where Renard is concerned." He shook his head. "You care about him, don't you?"

Andine flushed to his eyebrows. "Yes, monsieur."

"Oh, don't be embarrassed. Nothing wrong with it. Maybe if more people cared about each other, we wouldn't be continually at each other's throats." Jake flicked ash onto the floor. "Andine, if I asked you do to something for me—"

"I can do nothing that is against the law, monsieur." Andine drew himself up. "It is my sworn duty as a police officer to uphold the law."

"Don't worry. I'd never ask you to do anything that goes against the grain." Jake sized him up. "Maybe someday I might call up and ask you for a favor. Think you could do it?"

"It would depend on the favor, monsieur."

"It wouldn't be anything complicated." Jake drew on his cigarette. "Let's say I've located some fireworks… and I want you to set them off for me at a certain time. Think you could do that?"

Andine looked confused. "Fire… works, monsieur?"

When Paradise finally closed its doors around 4:00 a.m., Jake went upstairs to his apartment, shrugged out of his jacket, and unfastened his tie. He felt like he'd gone twenty rounds with Jimmy Braddock… or been run down by a truck.

Frederik Abaroa was sitting on the sofa, smoking a cigarette in silence. "He was here, wasn't he?"

"Yeah, he was here." Jake unbuttoned his shirt and rolled up his sleeves. He accepted the glass of whiskey Abaroa passed him and sank down onto the couch. "And then Renard came in, and boy, was that a pleasant scene."

Abaroa gazed at him with his large eyes, his expression compassionate. "I'm sorry, Jake." He patted Jake's arm. "Were you…?"

"Oh, he got the full blast, Nicolas did. We were kissing when he walked in. I tried to explain to him that it was just nostalgia, that we were just remembering what we'd had in Paris, but he wasn't buying it."

"Soon enough they will leave Maarif. An end to your troubles." Abaroa raised his glass in an ironic toast. "An end to all our troubles, I would hope, but it still leaves Danzig and the problem of Yvette and all the rest of it." He smirked. "Ahhh, Maarif, you dreadful cesspit of pain and misery! How I have missed your warm embrace."

"Careful," Jake said, "you're starting to sound like me." He pulled out a cigarette and accepted a light from Abaroa. "All I wanted out of Maarif was a simple life." Jake rubbed one hand over his face, scrubbing at his tired eyes. "I wanted to come here and run my whorehouse and live my life and forget all about Paris and Christophe Picard and the war and the rest of it. I had no intention of getting involved with anyone."

Abaroa nodded. "When did it happen?"

Jake sighed. "One night… we spent one night together… after Yvette was murdered."

Abaroa drew on his cigarette, the circle of light briefly illuminating his features. "Do you love him?"

"Oh, Christ… yes." Jake stretched his legs out in front of him. "He's a pain in my ass, and I can't live without him… he's been a pain in my ass from the first day I met him, and I love him. I'm in love with him." He sipped his drink. "It's stupid. I get that dumb little flutter in my guts when I see him, and I can't see him enough. I'm like a kid with his first crush. You know what that's like?"

Abaroa grinned. "Yes, Jake, I do." He swirled the contents of his glass. "Believe it or not, I have been in love myself a time or two."

Jake nodded. "Hey, what's the story with you and Christophe Picard, anyway?"

Abaroa shrugged. "He was my savior, in a manner of speaking. He took me off the streets and gave me a home, taught me to take care of myself." He glanced up at Jake. "I joined the Resistance because of him… because I wanted to make him proud of me."

"Is he?"

"I don't know. He has never said." The searchlight swept the room, brushing Abaroa's face. "I would do anything for Christophe Picard… anything at all."

*Yes, and you probably have.* "Does he know how you feel?"

Abaroa was momentarily surprised. "Oh, it's not like that. We were never… I never felt anything for him except the most platonic appreciation. He is a great man, and like great men everywhere, he is not easily distracted from his cause." He slugged the rest of his drink. "I think I will go to bed, if that is all right?"

"Sure." Jake laid his head against the back of the couch and smoked for a while, pondering the flash of lights across the ceiling and the strange shadows that resulted. He reached for the telephone, dialed a series of numbers, and listened to the click as the call was connected. "Are you still working?"

"Of course, I'm still working. This place has fallen into an utter shambles in my absence."

Jake knew Danzig or one of Danzig's aides was listening—the Nazis listened to all Jake's telephone calls. "I've got a bottle of that champagne you like. I think you should come and get it."

"Do you?"

"There's no rush." No sense in broadcasting it. "I'll keep it for you. You can pick it up tomorrow."

"Fine." There was a click and the line went dead. Jake poured himself another two fingers of whiskey and sat back. He lit another cigarette and smoked, listening to the rustle of the wind in the palms outside his window. Five minutes passed, perhaps ten, and then a car stopped outside. He listened carefully, measuring the cadence of the footsteps moving up the back stairs. Jake leaned out and opened the door to admit a hatless Renard, disheveled-looking and without his injured arm in a sling. "You came." His heart was thumping in his chest like a demented jackrabbit.

"Jake, Jake…." Renard leaned close. "You really do talk too much." He claimed Jake's mouth in a bruising kiss, pulling him close with his one good arm. "Now shut up," he hissed, "and take me to bed."


Stripped and gloriously nude, they came together in the middle of the bed, arms tight around each other. Jake took Renard's mouth in a savage, blistering kiss, and Renard groaned.

"You," Renard whispered when his mouth was free. "I have wanted nothing but you for as long as I can remember."

Their bodies meshed and limbs entwined, roving mouths licking and sucking, gently biting and soothing the tiny hurts. Renard shivered when Jake's hot mouth closed over the head of his cock and sucked him in. He clenched his fists and bit his lip to keep from crying out, and contented himself with murmuring an endless stream of nonsense phrases, half in French and half in English.

Jake mouthed Renard's balls while his hand slowly worked Renard's cock, sliding the pliable foreskin over the head and back in an endless, maddening rhythm.

Renard, flushed and sweaty, felt his toes curl under, and he reached for Jake and stayed him. "Wait." He rolled Jake onto his back and, bending low, licked the swollen cockhead. Jake's body jumped, and he moaned. "You are so beautiful," Renard murmured. "So beautiful when you are like this, my darling, all your defenses laid bare."

"Please." Jake's voice was strangled. "For God's sake, will you just—"

"*Un moment.*" Renard smiled against Jake's flat stomach. "All in good time, my darling."

Jake reached to clasp a hand around the back of Renard's neck. "I just want you."

"And you shall have me, but not just yet." Renard slipped a hand into the pocket of his discarded jacket and took out a small bottle of oil. With Jake lying face down, Renard smoothed the oil into the taut muscles of Jake's strong back, his hands moving in circles. He drizzled a thin stream of oil onto the rounded buttocks and rubbed a little harder. Jake's legs parted in a wordless invitation. Renard's slender fingers dipped between the muscled mounds and circled close to the puckered entrance—hesitated—then slid in.

Jake whimpered and raised his hips, pushing back onto Renard's fingers. "Oh *God,* Nicky, fuck me."

Renard fumbled with the bottle as his entire body flushed with wanton heat. He poured oil into the palm of his hand and rubbed himself, coating his cock. The tendons stood out on his neck, and he was sweating as he positioned himself at Jake's entrance. "Jake, my dear, are you sure?"

Jake swore at him and started up. "Nicky, if you—"

The rest of the sentence was lost as Renard's cock slid into him, pushing past the tight ring of muscle and into his heat. Jake's fingers groped for the pillow and crushed it, feathers breaking under his hands. Renard's cock was in him—that thought alone was enough to make him come—and Renard was fucking him. Renard, the man he had loved for as long as he could remember, the man whose face and memory had sustained him all those long and terrible months in prison…. Renard, who had never stopped searching for him until he found him and brought him home.

Renard thrust into him, and Jake pushed back. A storm of intense pleasure shivered through him, moving from the soles of his feet to the crown of his head. He angled his pelvis a little, and Renard's next stroke hit Jake's prostate, and the world went away, replaced by a blind, animal need. His hands dug into the mattress as they moved together, Renard's wiry body riding him, urging him forward until something deep inside Jake broke and washed over him in throbbing waves.

Renard pushed into him once more and then went absolutely still. He sobbed out his release against Jake's naked back and collapsed on him, his cheek against Jake's skin. "Jake, my boy… forgive me… lying on you…." He slipped away, rolled onto his back, and lay for a moment with his forearm over his eyes, completely spent.

Jake moved to lie next to him, his arm around Renard's waist, the skin there damp with perspiration. He nuzzled Renard's neck, leaned in, and captured his mouth. "You can lie on me any time, Nicky."

Renard chuckled. "Mmmmm. He's out there, you know."

"Danzig? Yeah, I know." Jake traced Renard's cheek with the ball of his thumb. "He's waiting for us."

"He won't come in. He's brazen, but not that brazen." Renard sighed. "Which means I shall have to go out to him."

"Not gonna happen," Jake said. "He'll shoot you as soon as you go through that door."

"You're not going out there," Renard said. "You can forget about it."

Jake leaned in and kissed Renard, and there was silence in the room for several long moments. "I love you," he murmured. "I should have said something before you went out into that damned desert, Nicolas."

"You really are a genius at self-excoriation," Renard said. "And by the way, I love you as well. I'm completely mad about you, in fact." He sighed. "Which does nothing to solve our problem of… him, out there."

"Oh, you can leave that to me," Jake said, grinning. "I've done a little bit of what you might call advance planning." He reached across Nicolas and lifted the receiver of the bedside phone. The sound of two clicks indicated he had been connected to the main exchange. "Give me Lieutenant Andine at the palais de justice," he said in French.

"Moment." There was a pause.

"Guillaume, that you? This is Jake Plenty. Yeah, I need you to do something for me…. No, no, it's fine. No, you'll like this…."

# CHAPTER
# NINE

Christophe Picard looked up at the tap on his hotel room door.

Maartje was sitting just across the room, quietly reading a book and trying to pretend her own anxiety wasn't eating her alive. "Christophe, the door."

"I know, darling, I'll get it." He rose and went to the door, opened it a crack, and peered through. "My God," he breathed, "is it really you?"

"Yes" came a distinctive voice from the other side. "Now open the damned door." Frederik Abaroa slipped into the room as noiselessly as a cat and bowed to Maartje. "Good evening, madame. I trust I find you well?"

Maartje stood, the book falling unheeded to the floor. "Monsieur Abaroa!" Her hands flew to her mouth. "We thought you were in—"

"Forgive me, madame. I heard about Captain Renard and felt it prudent to return. I was worried that our plan might not be successful. I hope I do not presume too much."

Picard grinned. "How far did you get?"

"Oran." Abaroa chuckled. "But what is a little distance between friends?" He seemed genuinely pleased to see them and not at all put out at having to return. "Now, then." He took a folded sheet of paper out of his trouser pocket and lit a cigarette. "If I could have your undivided attention…."

"I don't understand," Maartje said, once Abaroa had explained it to them. "How is this supposed to work?"

"It's not complicated, really," Abaroa said. "I am going to drive you both to the airport, and you are going to board the plane for Lisbon."

Maartje dimpled. "That would be lovely—if only it could happen that way."

Abaroa pouted, pretending to be hurt. "But it will happen that way!"

"Oh?" Picard leaned over the sheet of paper, examining the rather complicated flow chart Abaroa had painstakingly drawn. "And what about Major Danzig and his friends?"

"Oh, don't be afraid of that." Abaroa grinned. "Captain Renard and Monsieur Jake are making sure that Danzig and his aide remain outside Jake's apartment. They are waiting for Jake. Well, really they are waiting for Captain Renard, but who am I to quibble at trifles, hmm?" He lit a fresh cigarette. "The rest of the Nazis are going to be kept very busy. Lieutenant Andine will see to it. I believe—" He checked his wristwatch. "—he is arranging a little, shall we say, diversion for them, even as we speak." Abaroa shrugged theatrically. "With so much of their attention focused elsewhere, they won't have time to look toward the airport."

"Are you certain this… plan of yours… will work?" Picard didn't seem convinced.

"Not really." Abaroa shrugged. "But what is life without a little risk, hmm?"

Picard moved to the window and peered out, careful to keep himself out of the line of sight. There was something dark and dreadful twisting in his stomach, something that told him this was fruitless, that all of it would come to nothing, that everything would fail and he would disappear, blotted out of life like a mistake. "Maartje." He beckoned her over and wrapped an arm around her. "My dear, it occurs to me that I might not make it out of this war alive."

Abaroa bent over his makeshift map and pretended to ignore them.

"Christophe, don't say that." Maartje clung to him. "My darling, we have come through so much together. Surely this last step—"

"You must listen." He held her shoulders and made her look at him. "I have made provisions for you."

Maartje began to cry. "Christophe, please, don't say such things. It frightens me to hear you talk this way."

"There is no time." His voice frayed and broke a little on the last word. "Do you remember Jan, who worked at the bank? Tall Jan, with the red hair?"

The girl nodded.

"Ask Jan to give you the contents of my safety deposit box. There's some money there and an insurance policy. You will be all right."

"Christophe, I refuse to believe that anything will happen to you." She dried her eyes and raised her head to look at him. "Let's not speak about it. Monsieur Abaroa is waiting on us."

Abaroa bowed his head. "Madame, I am at your service." Her face had the look of a hunted animal. Abaroa had seen it many times before. It was the expression of someone who had seen what would be—and accepted it. He respected her for this. "War is hell," he murmured, and grinned.

"Now, give me a cigarette." Maartje straightened her skirt. "And let us see what this Major Danzig has in mind for us."


AROUND HALF an hour after Jake Plenty made the phone call to the palais de justice, a series of loud booms were heard off in the distance.

Renard leapt up from a light doze. "What the devil is that?"

"If I'm right—and I'm pretty sure I am—that'll be the Nazis."

Renard froze. "The Nazis are bombing Maarif?"

"Oh, no, Nicolas—sorry about that. Didn't mean to scare you." Jake smiled around a cigarette he was lighting. "No, that's Guillaume Andine you're hearing, Nicolas, my dear. Yeah, he got hold of some… well, maybe I shouldn't tell you. But he's giving the Germans something to think about." He paused, his head cocked to the sound of shouts just outside his window. "Oh, and that'd be Major Danzig and his boys. Yeah, they should be leaving right about now."

As if on cue, the big car roared to life, Danzig screaming to be heard above the powerful engine.

"Oh, Jake." Renard grabbed him by the back of the neck and pulled him close. "You sneaky bastard." The kiss—torrid, sensual—was interrupted by the abrupt shrilling of the telephone.

Jake put out his cigarette and lifted the receiver. At the same time, the ever-present sweep of the German searchlight went out like the blink of a shuttered eyelid. "Hello?"

Renard sat up on the edge of the bed and reached for his clothes.

"What?" Jake's face went very still. Renard stood and began to dress. "I see. Well, that changes things." He laid the receiver back in its cradle. "The Nazis have blockaded the airport. No flights in or out."


"IT SHOULD be a very simple matter. If you will permit me"—Abaroa went to the telephone—"I must make a quick telephone call. Don't worry, I will reimburse the hotel. It's really nothing, only a moment or two." He listened as the call was connected and then began speaking rapidly in French. "I ought to have foreseen this." He hung up and turned to Picard. "I am afraid, Monsieur Salazar, that there has been a change in our plans."

Picard blinked, and Maartje made some small noise beside him. "Yes?"

"Major Danzig has closed the airport." Abaroa rubbed at his forehead in a distracted manner. "A battalion of Germans arrived from Vichy quite unexpectedly. Yes, very unexpectedly." He spread his hands, a gesture of utter helplessness. "I am afraid your escape route has been… cut off."

"Cut off?" Maartje gripped Picard's arm with both hands. "Christophe, what will we do? We have to get out of Maarif. If you stay, they will capture you. You'll end up in a concentration camp."

"Please, my dear." Picard patted her, his mind clearly elsewhere. "Frederik, do you think it is possible that we might—the train… what about the train?"

Abaroa shook his head. "I do not know, monsieur. In theory—"

"Never mind your theory!" Picard was unreasoning, wild. "We have to get out of here. There is a price on my head, on all our heads. I cannot afford to linger in Maarif!" Maartje reached for him, but he shook her off. "Good God, man! What sort of a game are you playing? I have spent the last few months in hiding, creeping from one neutral country to the other, always in sight of the German lines, always worried that at any moment I might be discovered. Then a chance meeting with you in Algiers, and what do you say to me? 'Come to Maarif. It is the safest point of embarkation to America.' I do as you say. I bring my wife. I take the most extravagant risks, and for what? To be stopped at the last moment?" He cursed Abaroa, raved at him, spittle flying from his lips. "All this time and all this planning, and for what? Am I to be lost to my cause because of your bungling?"

There was silence, save for Picard's rasping breath and Maartje's stifled sobs. Abaroa forced himself to speak quietly. "I… regret that unforeseen complications have occurred."

Picard rounded on him. "You *regret*?" He swiped at Abaroa and was suddenly stopped by Maartje.

"Christophe!" She grabbed his arm, furious. "That's enough."

Picard folded down onto the bed and hid his face in his hands.

"Monsieur Abaroa, is there any chance at all that the railway might afford us an escape?" Maartje took up her purse and opened it. "I have a little money. Perhaps you can purchase tickets for us under assumed names. There must be somewhere we can go."

Picard's voice was muffled by his hands. "There is nowhere we can go."

"But are you sure? Perhaps there is—"

"There is nowhere!" He roared at her. "Do you not understand me? This is where it ends. Right here in this stinking desert hell hole!"

Abaroa grimaced: THE HERO PICARD. "I will get the tickets." He pressed Maartje's hand. "Madame, do not trouble yourself. If this is how the trip must be accomplished, well...." He shrugged and smiled his luminous smile. "*Inshallah*, madame."


"HE WAS in Danzig's pay." Renard slid into the car beside Jake and slammed the door. "The Priest.... Danzig hired him even before he came to Maarif and kept him on retainer, just in case he needed extra muscle. A crazed madman you can summon out of the desert. How very convenient." He shook his head. "Poor Yvette." He braced himself against the dashboard as Jake took the next two corners at a precarious angle. "Jake, you're a horrible driver."

"Nicolas, you know I love you, but if you don't shut up...." Jake took the next corner on two wheels, and Renard shuddered. "So, now Picard is going to try his luck with the railway? Him and her?"

"Oh yeah. Abaroa said he'd fix it."

"Well, let's hope we can trust the boy to bring it off." Renard glanced at his watch. "A quarter to midnight. This is devilish timing... devilish timing." He gazed through the windscreen at the night. "So much for Salazar's miraculous disappearance." He turned to Jake. "You realize our proverbial goose is cooked, don't you? We'll have to leave after this. We'll have made Maarif too hot to hold us, Jake." He hesitated, then plunged on. "Ali... I can't leave him here. Jake, we'll have to take him with us. I can't leave him."

Jake canted a sidelong look at him. "He's your son, isn't he?"

Renard's heart thumped in his chest. "Yes, Jake. He is."

"That woman you told me about... the one in Dover?"

Renard nodded, but his gaze was directed inward, seeing something Jake could not. "Yes, Jake."

"Jesus." Jake digested that in silence for a moment. "The kid... does he know?"

"I don't know. We've never discussed it. I was in the Legion when I got word from England that the woman who had been caring for him had died. His own mother died in childbirth. I never *really* knew for sure, if I was Ali's father… not till later."

Jake nodded. "Huh" was all he said.

"Jake, I meant what I said. We have to leave."

"Don't I know it." Jake sighed, thinking of Paradise. What would his girls do without him? And what about Andy and Piet and the rest of his staff? "Aww, I was getting sick of this place anyway."

"And where do you suppose we'll go, hmm?" Renard raised an eyebrow. "Maybe skip off to America with the Picards?"

"I wasn't planning on it," Jake said grimly. "There's nothing in America for me."

"Ah." Renard nodded. "Well, there are plenty of Free French garrisons about. The desert is honeycombed with them. We've merely to spin ourselves in a circle and head off in any direction."

"Free French, eh?" Jake sounded as if he were giving it some serious thought. "What'll we do?"

"Fight," Renard said. "We fight, Jake. We win this war. Sound good?"

"No," Jake said, "it sounds crummy." He turned down a side street, scooted through a narrow alleyway, and emerged on the other side of a mosque. The railway station was directly ahead, close enough to see. "Well," Jake remarked to no one in particular, "I didn't plan on living forever anyway." He pulled the car up next to the station, and they got out.

The late train to Algiers sat waiting, its engines idling quietly by the platform. The air was heavy with the stink of coal and petrol. Two robed, hooded figures, both clad in traditional *djebellas*, detached themselves from the shadows at the side of the platform and came forward: Christophe and Maartje Picard.

Frederik Abaroa emerged from inside the station, saw Jake and Renard, and nodded. "I apologize for getting you out of bed, Monsieur le Capitaine." Abaroa wasn't quite smirking. "I trust I have not entirely ruined your rest?"

"This is highly irregular." Renard's hands toyed with his Sam Browne. "And very dangerous." He cursed quietly in French. "You chose quite a time to be the hero, Abaroa." He jerked his chin at the two robed figures on the platform. "Are they ready?"

"As ready as they will ever be, monsieur." Abaroa patted his shirt pocket. "I will go with them as far as Algiers. An escort of sorts."

"Mmm. They'll need it."

Abaroa had just motioned Picard and Maartje forward when a big car barreled toward them, juddering over the bumps in the road much too fast, with Danzig at the wheel. He was demented: his face bone-white, his teeth clenched. "Stop! No one is leaving here! No one!" He screeched to a stop, leaped out, and strode toward them with his henchmen in tow. The blond man who had volunteered to carry Danzig's suitcases looked particularly put out at having to dispatch a group of spies—perhaps he'd been asleep when Danzig's summons came. "Step away from the platform. No one is leaving here tonight."

"Not correct, monsieur." Abaroa's hand delved into his jacket and came out holding a lethal little snub-nosed revolver. "You will stay exactly where you are."

A third vehicle came out of the darkness: a police car, with several of Renard's most trusted officers aboard. They made to get out of the car, but Renard motioned for them to stay where they were.

"You are all enemies of the Reich!" Danzig stalked toward the Picards. "The concentration camp for all of you! You will die for this! I swear, you will—"

"Perhaps you did not hear me." Abaroa's soft voice seemed to carry for miles. "But I told you to stay exactly where you are."

Danzig's hand came up holding a Luger. He waved it at the two robed figures, motioning them forward. "You will surrender yourselves immediately into my custody."

Picard lowered his hood, exposing his face to Danzig. He moved forward into the light, hands raised at shoulder level. "Here I am, Herr Danzig. I only ask that you spare my wife. You have no quarrel with her."

"No, Herr Salazar, I have no quarrel with her." Danzig tilted his head to the side and regarded the Resistance leader with something like curiosity. "Mostly, my quarrel is with you. You have escaped me once. You will not escape me a second time."

The shot, when it came, was unexpected, unbelievable.

The Luger jumped in Danzig's hand and a patch of red bloomed on the front of Picard's robes. He staggered forward, arms outstretched toward Danzig. The Luger leaped twice more, bullets crashing into Picard's shoulder and his forehead. At such close range, Danzig could hardly miss. He advanced another step, and it was his undoing: Abaroa's arm seemed to stretch into infinity as he leaned forward, eyes narrowed, his whole attention concentrated on Danzig. There was a short, sharp retort from Abaroa's tiny gun, and Danzig stopped, his face contorting into an almost comical expression of surprise. His mouth opened, and he struggled to speak for a moment, then crumpled soundlessly to the ground. A dark pool spread out from the back of his head.

The blond man shouted something and started forward, but was abruptly restrained by one of Renard's officers. Maartje was kneeling by the body of her husband, holding his head in her lap. Jake went to her and murmured something no one else could hear.

"Well," Renard said dryly, "Major Danzig has been shot and that's too bad." He gestured at Andine. "Take them into custody, all of them, and have them charged with conspiracy to murder."

Andine blinked. "Murder?"

"Yes. You know it's a terrible thing when a group of men decide to mutiny. I daresay Major Danzig never saw it coming. Take them, Andine."

Andine nodded. "Oui, monsieur."

"What will you do?" Jake asked Maartje. "You could come with us, you know. Nicky and me, we'd keep an eye on you, make sure nothing happens to you."

The girl shook her head. "No. Thank you, Mr. Plenty, but no." She stood and smoothed down her robes. "I am wanted in America and I am getting on that train." She gazed down at her hands, twisting her wedding ring on her finger. "He would have wanted that. He would want me to continue his work." She turned shining eyes to him. "That's what I will do, Monsieur Plenty."

*Good God, he's infected you completely.* "If that's what you want."

"It is." She took his hand. "Thank you for everything you tried to do for us."

"I'm not the one you should thank," Jake said. "Freddie Abaroa put himself in harm's way for Christophe."

"Monsieur Abaroa knows how much I appreciate the things he did." She let go of his hand and stepped back. "Could you do one last thing for me? I hate to ask."

Jake's throat was suddenly tight with unshed tears, and he didn't really know why. "I'll make sure he has a decent burial."

"Thank you." Then she was gone.

"Think Mrs. Picard will survive the war?" Renard laid his good hand on Jake's back.

"Oh, I think so." Jake lit a cigarette. "Some people are like that."

"Yes," Renard said. "Some people are." He stepped back from the platform as the conductor's whistle blew. "What about you, Jake?"

"What about me?" Jake wrapped an arm around his shoulders, careful of Renard's wound.

"I daresay you wish you were on that train and on your way back to America."

"No, Nicolas, this time you're wrong." Jake walked him back to the car. "I don't wish I was anywhere except where I am right now."

"Oh, dear. Someone really has chipped a hole in that stone heart of yours." Renard slid into the backseat, and Jake slid in after him.

"Somebody did." It felt good to admit it. It felt right. "Little French guy. It's the damnedest thing you ever saw."

"Mm. Let me guess: and now you're all ready to redeem yourself, bid farewell to your sinful ways, and… what?" Renard was momentarily alarmed. "Jake, I confess, I don't know how this story ends."

Andine started the car, and they pulled away from the tarmac. "Monsieur le Capitaine, I am blind as a bat," Andine said. "Insofar as I can see anything involving yourself and Monsieur Jake."

Jake chuckled. "That's good to know, Guillaume." He took Renard into his arms gently. "How'd we get here, Nicky?"

"I haven't the faintest." Renard turned his face up for Jake's kiss. "But I'm not sorry." He laid his cheek against Jake's shoulder. "I'm not sorry at all."

# EPILOGUE

In the end, Abaroa supposed it went off as well as could have been expected. Christophe Picard was buried in a nice little Coptic cemetery near the outskirts of Maarif, and Maartje Picard went safely to America. Someone—probably the railway staff, although no one cared enough to find out—cleaned up what was left of Major Danzig. Guillaume Andine distinguished himself by bringing in Yvette's murderer, who confessed under interrogation that he had been hired by Danzig. Abaroa caught the train to Oran and waited there for his orders. Nicolas Renard and Jake Plenty left Maarif with Renard's houseboy, Ali, and the three men made their way back into the fighting.

And finally, after the war was over, Jake brought Renard back to Paris. He took Renard down the Rue Pigalle and found Madame Fragonard's, which had enjoyed a roaring trade during the war, but which had now sadly fallen into disarray. They learned from Pierre, one of Madame Fragonard's boys, that Madame died not long after the Germans had marched into the city, ostensibly of cancer, but many who had known her maintained she had really died of a broken heart.

"She never got over it, Jacob. The day the Germans came, with their trucks and their big guns, something inside of her went away."

He and Renard bought bread and wine and sat by the Seine, watching the boats go up and down. "Is it like you remembered?" Jake passed the bottle to Renard.

"Ah, Jacob, nothing is ever exactly as one remembers it. I'm not a man who puts much faith in nostalgia." Renard took a swig and passed the bottle back. "I'd rather live in the moment, with a happy anticipation of the future."

"Does…." It was hard to say, even after everything they'd been through. "Does that future include me?"

Renard gazed at him. There were new lines around Renard's eyes, and the furrows beside his mouth had deepened. The rigors of war hung on his shoulders like an invisible garment. "I love you, Jake, with all my heart and soul and everything that is in me. If that's too romantic for your pragmatic American soul, then I—"

Jake leaned in and quickly kissed him.

"We'll be arrested." Twin spots of red burned in Renard's cheeks.

"Hasn't been illegal in France for a long time." Jake was grinning like a fool. "That Bonaparte guy took care of it."

"You really are the most irritating man."

"But you love me."

"Yes, Jake. I love you. And I should like to spend the rest of my life with you, if you'll have me."

Jake raised the bottle, toasting him. "That goes double for me, Nicolas." He drank deeply. "That goes double for me."

# APPENDIX

THE TREVOR PROJECT

The Trevor Project operates the only nationwide, around-the-clock crisis and suicide prevention helpline for lesbian, gay, bisexual, transgender and questioning youth. Every day, The Trevor Project saves lives through its free and confidential helpline, its website, and its educational services. If you or a friend are feeling lost or alone, call The Trevor Helpline. If you or a friend are feeling lost, alone, confused, or in crisis, please call The Trevor Helpline. You'll be able to speak confidentially with a trained counselor 24/7.

The Trevor Helpline: 866-488-7386

On the Web: http://www.thetrevorproject.org/

THE GAY MEN'S DOMESTIC VIOLENCE PROJECT

Founded in 1994, The Gay Men's Domestic Violence Project is a grassroots, nonprofit organization founded by a gay male survivor of domestic violence and developed through the strength, contributions, and participation of the community. The Gay Men's Domestic Violence Project supports victims and survivors through education, advocacy, and direct services. Understanding that the serious public health issue of domestic violence is not gender-specific, we serve men in relationships with men, regardless of how they identify, and stand ready to assist them in navigating through abusive relationships.

GMDVP Helpline: 800.832.1901 On the Web: http://gmdvp.org/

## THE GAY & LESBIAN ALLIANCE AGAINST DEFAMATION/GLAAD EN ESPAÑOL

The Gay & Lesbian Alliance Against Defamation (GLAAD) is dedicated to promoting and ensuring fair, accurate and inclusive representation of people and events in the media as a means of eliminating homophobia and discrimination based on gender identity and sexual orientation.

On the Web: http://www.glaad.org

J.S. COOK was born and raised on the island of Newfoundland. She holds a B.A. and an M.A. in English Language and Literature and a B.Ed in post-secondary education. She makes her home in St. John's, Newfoundland, with her husband Paul, and Lola, her spoiled rotten dogter.

J.S. Cook also writes as JoAnne Soper-Cook.
Twitter: twitter.com/jsopercook
Website: joannesopercook.net

Enjoy historicals? Check out

Keep reading for an excerpt!

# The Lonely War

By Alan Chin

The realities of war are brutal for any man, but for a Buddhist like Andrew Waters, they're unthinkable. And reconciling his serene nature with the savagery of World War II isn't the only challenge Andrew faces. First, he must overcome the deep prejudice his half-Chinese ancestry evokes from his shipmates, a feat he manages by providing them with the best meals any destroyer crew ever had. Then he falls in love with his superior officer, and the two men struggle to satisfy their growing passion within the confines of the military code of conduct. In a distracted moment, he reveals his sexuality to the crew, and his effort to serve his country seems doomed.

When the ship is destroyed, Andrew and the crew are interned in Changi, a notorious Japanese POW camp. In order to save the life of the man he loves, Andrew agrees to become the commandant's whore. He uses his influence with the commandant to help his crew survive the hideous conditions, but will they understand his sacrifice or condemn him as a traitor?

Available from DSP Publications
www.dsppublications.com

# CHAPTER ONE

*March 20, 1941—0800 hours*

IN THE Spring of 1941, the Japanese army surged across the border from China to extend their bloody campaign to all of Southeast Asia. As war crept south, the French, English, and American foreigners scattered throughout Indochina hastened to Saigon, where they boarded ocean liners bound for their homelands. Meanwhile, the Japanese army massed at the outskirts of Saigon, poised for another victorious assault. The city held its breath as the invaders prepared for the onslaught.

Andrew Waters pursued his father across a bustling wharf, still wearing his boarding-school uniform and clutching a bamboo flute.

The ship that loomed before him was a floating city, mammoth, with numerous passenger decks topped by two massive exhaust stacks muddying the sky. It had berthed at the port of Saigon—an inland port on a tributary of the Mekong—for a full week. Now, Andrew saw the crew scurrying to get underway.

The wharf trembled slightly. Andrew heard the rat-tat-tat of gunfire over the sirens blaring from the center of the city.

Andrew's father sported a tussore silk suit of superlative cut and a Panama hat tilted so that the brim hid his right eye. His tall figure marched purposefully toward the black-and-white behemoth, and his normally long gait lengthened with a noticeable desperation.

Andrew, who was nearly eighteen, paused while panting from an acute nervy rush. He searched the sky for planes. They were still beyond his field of vision, but the drone of bombers echoed through the cloud cover. The rumble of explosions grew loud and the air carried the faint stench of sulfur.

He hurried on, jostling through a mélange of beings: Caucasians dressed in fine Western clothes (like his father), rich Chinese in their silks, merchants in long-sleeved jackets, coolies wearing only tattered shorts. Voices around him were shouting while the harsh twang of a military band playing "Auld Lang Syne" vaulted above that unbridled fusion of humanity.

Behind Andrew trotted an aged wisp of a monk who wore the traditional orange robes and held a string of wooden prayer beads. Each bead was the size of a marble and had the chalky gray coloring of Mekong silt. The monk's thumb deliberately ticked past each bead, one after another, like a timer counting down the seconds. Behind the monk came the porters carrying four steamer trunks.

At the gangway, his father told Andrew to make his good-bye, and he sprinted up the ramp with the porters in tow.

Surrounded by a press of bodies, the youth reverently embraced the monk. The old man's arms wrapped around Andrew and drew him nearer. The monk's breath tickled his neck, which helped to dissolve his anxieties.

Using the native tongue of South China, he whispered, "Master, I'll come home as soon as I can."

The monk's face contracted, as if Andrew had posed a difficult question. "Andrew, war and time will whisk away everything that you love. This is our farewell."

The youth wiped away a tear that broke free from his almond-shaped eyes and slid down his amber-colored cheek. "Master, I will remember everything you have taught me."

"You will forget my lessons, Andrew. Such is the nature of youth. But remember this: you are American by birth, so they will surely draft you. On the battlefield, resist the hate that is born from fear. Nurture only love in your heart. To love all beings is Buddha-like and transcends us from the world of pain, for love is the highest manifestation of life. To experience love's full bounty is life's only purpose, so tread the moral path before you and sacrifice yourself to love. All else is folly, a dream of the ego."

"Master, I do not understand about sacrificing myself to love."

The old monk's eyes opened wide and his lips spread into a grin. "Meditate on what I have said. Understanding will come when you are ready."

The monk methodically bundled his string of beads into a ball, roughly the size and shape of a monkey's skull, and forced them into Andrew's left pant pocket. "Keep these beads to remind yourself of our time together."

The pressure against Andrew's thigh felt awkward. As the monk pulled way, Andrew became distracted, thinking of how fortunate this man was to be wise and compassionate in the midst of the impending carnage. Andrew realized that it took impeccable courage to maintain one's morality during perilous times, courage that he himself did not possess. He had always assumed that he would live a quiet, studious, and spiritual life under this old monk's guardianship and eventually become the old man who stood before him. But that image, of course, had been shattered when war turned the world on its head. Now all Andrew could think about was getting on that ship and sailing to safety, if such a thing existed.

The ship's whistle cut the air, long and terrible, and loud enough to be heard throughout the city. The monk pressed his hands together in front of his forehead and bowed, silently, with finality.

Another blast from the ship's whistle sent the youth running up the gangway, leaving the earthy world of South China behind. He joined his father on the first-class deck. Entombed in steel—underfoot, heavy riveted plates of metal curved into walls—Andrew jammed together with the other passengers at the railing, peering down at the apprehensive faces. Their body heat added to the stifling temperature. Sweat dribbled down his neck. He had to gasp to get enough air.

Lines fell away; the gangway was hauled aboard. Tugs pushed the ship into the middle of the channel and withdrew, leaving the ship to the whim of the current.

Andrew stared straight down at the seemingly dense, opaque surface of the river. It reflected the cloudy sky, making the water seem gray rather than its usual brown, with yellowish streaks of oil running with the current. To Andrew, the flat, moving surface seemed strangely alive, carrying him along, muscling him downstream, as if it was some overwhelming force whose motives he could only guess at.

On the dock, Asian women held their infants over their heads for a last look. Handkerchiefs waved. The band played on.

Andrew saw the first planes against the darkening sky, droning above the city. Explosions grew even louder. From his perch on the first-class deck, he saw sections of the city erupting. He turned northeast, toward his boarding school. Flames. That entire section of the city was engulfed in fire, as if Hell had opened its mouth to swallow it whole.

"Clifford," he whispered.

A searing stab of regret lodged in his chest. He had been forced to abandon the object of his adolescent love, and he imagined himself dashing through the chaotic streets to reach the boarding school. There was still time, he thought. They could disappear into the forest. They could live on, together. He wanted to perform that fatal act of love, but he wondered if he could muster the courage to defy his father.

Reluctantly (at least it felt that way to him), he climbed the railing to dive overboard, because he realized that the love he shared with Clifford wasn't a trifling adolescent crush at all, but rather a deep and consuming love—a love that had somehow lost itself in the joys of youth, like water in dry sand, and was only now understood.

His father pulled him back, forcing him to stay and suffer what felt like an unquenchable loss. Locked in his father's embrace, he entered a narrow canyon of desolation, knowing that the days and hours and minutes ahead would be heartbreaking and that he might not be strong enough to endure it.

The ship's siren sounded three blasts for its farewell salute. The engines throbbed and propellers chewed the river. The noise swelled to a din like the ending of the world.

The passengers on deck could no longer hide their sorrow. Everyone wept, not only those people parting but the onlookers as well; even the dockhands and porters shed tears.

The ship launched itself downstream under its own power as the military band played "The Star-Spangled Banner."

To Andrew, the orange-robed figure crushed within the throng on the dock seemed at odds with the fires raging across the city. He now fully understood the monk's words—that war would steal everything he loved. A way of life, their way of life, had perished. Pain flooded his whole being, like a baby prematurely ripped from its protective womb.

He pulled away from his father and staggered further along the deck to cry without letting his father see. He positioned himself at the rail, one arm folded around a steel support beam and his face pressed against the hot metal.

People on the wharf seemed to hesitate, then regretfully turned and scurried away. He watched the smudge of orange, scarcely visible and standing at the edge of the pier, utterly still, quiescent, until the harbor faded from view and the land disappeared as well, slowly swallowed beneath the curve of the earth.

# CHAPTER TWO

*April 18, 1942—0700 hours*

FOUR SAILORS toiled under the deadweight of their seabags—marching two up, two back—with their heads bowed to avoid the equatorial sun's glare. They trailed the executive officer of their newly assigned ship, who led them away from the orderly grid of gravel roads and Quonset huts that made up the Viti Levu Naval Repair Facility, toward the harbor where several warships rested at anchor. Each sailor had his seabag slung over his right shoulder and carried a folded cot under his left arm.

The full brunt of the sun hammered Seaman Andrew Waters. Sweat turned his dungaree uniform a dark shade of blue, and the muggy air made his breathing feel like ingesting lukewarm seawater.

To take his mind off the heat, Andrew studied the confident gait of Lieutenant Nathan Mitchell. The exec's khaki uniform was freshly pressed; its only blemish was a small sweat stain under each armpit. A green canvas belt hugged his waist, and from it hung a canteen over his left hip and a holster over his right. The holster partially concealed a Browning .45 automatic.

Mitchell was lean for his six-foot-one height. Andrew thought his bronzed skin and fawn-colored hair made him appear too young for his rank of lieutenant. Andrew guessed the officer's age to be about ten years older than himself—twenty-eight or nine—and at that moment, Mitchell whistled a happy tune on this excruciatingly hot morning.

By the time they passed the Port Director's office, sweat streamed off Andrew's forehead, and he felt his remaining strength drain from his legs, making it nearly impossible to carry his burden. I've failed again, he thought. Time after time he had struggled to pull his weight with his shipmates, but his slim frame was not built to endure physical hardship. At home he used his sharp intelligence to prove his worth, but the US Navy only valued brute strength and moronic obedience from its seamen. In this theater of fighting men, he was a failure.

He would have loved to drop his seabag and sail home to the boarding school to bury himself in literature, music, and mathematics. But that was not an option. So he swallowed hard, making a last-ditch effort to keep up with the others.

He managed a dozen more steps along the dock before he saw, through sweat-blurred vision, Seaman Grady Washington begin to stagger like a drunkard and stumble backward. Andrew dropped his gear and jumped to break Grady's fall, grabbing the young Negro from behind. The deadweight of his unconscious shipmate drove them both to the dock.

Sprawled under Washington, crushed against the wooden planks, it seemed as though a strong man had pinned him, holding him prisoner. It felt like a personal affront.

Andrew yelled to Lieutenant Mitchell, who still held a tune on his lips.

Mitchell turned to stare at the fallen sailors. He pointed to one of the other men and said with an authoritative voice, "Hudson, help Waters carry that man to the shade."

Petty Officer Third Class Joe Hudson, a swarthy sailor dressed in frayed dungarees, lowered his gear to the dock. He grabbed Grady under both armpits and muscled the sailor to the shade beside the Port Director's office. The lieutenant followed as he unhooked the canteen from his webbed belt. He told Andrew to hold Grady's head up while he knelt and poured water over the comatose sailor's nappy head.

Grady coughed, his eyelids fluttered.

With the officer kneeling only two feet way, for the first time Andrew was able to furtively study the lieutenant's face. His heartbeat quickened. The man's cheeks were attractively sunburnt and supported a straight nose and powerful eyebrows. Andrew detected a keen intelligence simmering behind those eyes, which were clear and discerning and the color of pale jade. Their intensity startled Andrew. He inhaled sharply, catching a whiff of the officer's scent. Beneath the pleasant odor of talcum powder, he discovered the aroma of sweat-moistened skin.

Andrew tried to look away, but he couldn't help but follow the path of a bead of sweat sliding from under the officer's hat, making its way along the reddish cheek and strong jaw, where it clung to that beautifully sun-kissed skin. Andrew felt himself drawn to the officer like the moon draws water.

Grady's eyelids popped open and his eyes rolled around in their sockets like loose marbles. His lips trembled with unrealized words, as if he might possibly have a speech disorder.

Mitchell pressed the canteen to the black sailor's lips, trickled water into the pink cavity, and poured more water over his head.

"You fainted from the heat, sailor," Mitchell said. "Happens all the time."

"You'd think a jungle bunny would be used to the heat," Hudson quipped while mopping his shaved head with a purple handkerchief, "being from Africa and all."

Andrew glanced up, scrutinizing Petty Officer Hudson and Seaman John Stokes, who stood in the shade, casually watching the scene. Stokes was a Nebraska farm boy with strawberry-colored hair and a Milky Way of freckles scattered across his face. He carried himself with an ungainly youthfulness, as if he was still growing into his body. His pillbox hat was bleached an absolute white and tilted so far forward that it hid his eyebrows.

"Button that mouth, Hudson," Mitchell barked. "We don't tolerate racial slurs on the Pilgrim."

"Sir," Hudson replied, "does that include half Japs, too? I thought we was here to kill Japs."

"One more insulting remark and you're on report. Is that clear, sailor?"

"Aye, sir. Crystal."

It's starting already, Andrew thought. Okay, survival rule number one: never show fear. Rule number two: deflect opposing force by pulling your adversary off balance.

Andrew eased Grady's head onto the dock and stood to face Hudson. He swallowed. Hudson was built like a heavyweight prizefighter. His face revealed the bent bulb of a nose that had been crushed and remolded, a dished cheekbone, and scars over both eyes. His body looked distorted and menacing, and his swagger was common among the "old salts" who had a hard need to prove they were the stud bulls of the herds.

Andrew held him with an unflinching stare. "It's time you learned the difference between Japanese and Chinese," he said with a slight French accent. "For the record, I'm half Chinese, half American."

"Chinks and Japs is all the same," Hudson snarled. "They all smell yellow to me."

"The Chinese are our allies," Andrew said. "They've fought the Japanese on and off for over eight hundred years. Japan has been kicking America's butt for only, what, five months?"

Hudson sneered. "In the old Navy, we didn't put up with smart-mouth chinks and namby-pamby niggers. In the old navy you could trust the man next to you with your life. But those days is gone, and for a buffalo-head nickel I'd get the hell out this new Navy."

"That's it, Hudson," Mitchell said. "You're on report."

"Only a nickel?" Andrew dipped two fingers into the pocket of his dungaree pants and extracted a quarter. "Here's two bits. Tell the discharge officer to keep the change." He flung the coin at Hudson. It tumbled through the air, hitting the petty officer in the chest, dead center.

Hudson clenched a ham-like fist. "Sass me again, you yellow monkey, and I'll kick you bowlegged!"

"Can the bickering, right now." Lieutenant Mitchell stepped between them. "On my ship, we get along, do our jobs, and if anyone makes waves, I jump on them with both my size-twelve's kicking. Another word out of either of you and it will cost you your next five liberties. Understood?"

"Yes, sir," they sang out.

"Hudson and Stokes, wait at the whaleboat. Waters, help me get Washington on his feet."

Andrew knew he could safely confront Hudson with the lieutenant on hand, but even so, relief swept through his center like an ocean wave. This, he knew, was the first barrage of an ongoing battle, and once aboard ship, Mitchell wouldn't be conveniently on the spot to protect him.

Hudson and Stokes retrieved their gear and marched down the pier. Andrew pulled Grady to a sitting position.

Mitchell handed Grady his canteen. "Clear your head before you try to stand, sailor."

Grady clambered to his feet and handed the officer his canteen. "Thank you, suh," he drawled. "I reckon I'm fine now."

Andrew and Grady hoisted their gear and followed the lieutenant to the whaleboat nestled at the pier's head. Andrew admired the boat's functionally beautiful lines, with its broad beam and both ends sporting a sharp bow. The Navy still used these boats because they inspired confidence in a heavy sea and landing through rough surf.

Hudson sat on a thwart near the bow with Stokes behind him. Three oarsmen manned each side; a coxswain stood at the tiller. All seven dungaree-clad crewmen glared at Andrew and Grady as they passed their seabags to an oarsman. A facade of disbelief turning to anger spread over each face.

"What'd I tell you?" Hudson sneered.

The redheaded coxswain spit over the gunwale.

Grady climbed into the boat while Andrew gazed at the redhead standing at the tiller. The man's lips seemed too small for his mouth, stretched over teeth that were somewhat pointed and bared to the gums, like a rabid dog. Andrew's absentminded scrutiny of the stranger proved dangerous, because he suddenly realized that the redhead was staring back at him so aggressively that his intention was clearly to make an issue of the matter.

"Look alive, Waters," the lieutenant said.

Andrew dropped beside the lieutenant with his right shoulder pressed to Mitchell's left, their knees touching. They pushed off and were borne along by rowers. The boat seemed to fly over the blue-green plane. Andrew noticed the clocklike cadence of the oars, the rowers' labored breathing, and the faint scent of the lieutenant's sweat-moistened skin, still hovering under the pleasant aroma of talcum powder.

They passed a line of predators at anchor—destroyers, a cruiser, a submarine—all swarming with deckhands and welders and riveters, most of whom were stripped to the waist and covered with grime.

Andrew stared out over the bay. The morning was like true summer, with the sea smooth and bright under the sun and a slight breeze off the water to soften the heat's edge. He glanced at the horizon. A line of dark cumulus clouds galloped toward them from the southeast.

Mitchell shifted beside him. His eyes followed the young sailor's gaze. "You see it?"

Andrew no longer contemplated the oncoming squall. He felt the lieutenant next to him, heard the man's clear voice fuse with the sound of his own shallow breathing. His pulse thumped at his temples as he turned to gaze into those jade-green eyes. His mind floundered for a heartbeat before he said, "Should hit around sundown, sir."

Mitchell nodded.

Andrew's eyes widened as they approached his new ship, and his spirits sank. She lay low in the water, the USS Pilgrim, Destroyer #119. Her twenty thousand tons of steel was shaped like a knife—her forecastle rose high above the water from bow to bridge like a sturdy handle and fell sharply away to a low main deck that ran from conning tower to stern like a thin blade. Four smokestacks sprouted from her superstructure, their gaunt columns smudged the sky with black smoke. Andrew counted two bulky gun turrets with five-inch guns perched on her forecastle, a half dozen torpedo launchers along her amidships, and two stern-mounted depth-charge racks. She's an awesome mass of destructive power wrapped in gray steel.

A deeply spiritual young man, Andrew was about to board a ship whose sole purpose was to destroy human life. He felt his testicles draw close to his body as the Pilgrim grew large before him. He silently told himself that even on this death machine, he must stay true to his pacifist principles.

The whaleboat came to rest alongside a limp chain ladder hanging from the Pilgrim's quarterdeck. Mitchell scurried aboard, saluted the colors, and turned to supervise the gear being hoisted over the railing. A gaggle of sailors flocked to the afterdeck, all leaning over the railing cables to get a glimpse of the new men. A few catcalls cut the morning air, but most of the men simply glared down at Andrew.

He stood in the whaleboat with his legs spread for balance, his head rising above and falling below the level of the Pilgrim's main deck. He hesitated, studying the torpedo launchers along the amidships, before climbing the ladder with the awkwardness of a landsman. Here, then, was a final moment of perception before his surrender: the deadly gray hulk, the crew's defiant stares, the dark line of clouds advancing on him, and Mitchell's jade-colored eyes beckoning him aboard.

He stepped on deck by a deliberate act of will (it felt deliberate, although he was too numb to form thoughts), surrendering to his fate.

For a moment, still, nothing seemed different. It felt like another failure, as if he could still jump overboard, swim to shore, and all would be set right. But a brutish sailor wearing oily dungarees charged along the narrow deck, deliberately slamming into him with a beefy shoulder. Andrew stumbled over a tangled nest of air hoses, landing hard on his butt. The sailor snarled, "Stay the fuck out of my way, Jap-boy!"

Andrew's stomach folded in on itself as he realized this crew was roughly the same as the one on his last ship. He could feel their apprehension. He knew that he, and even Grady for that matter, would never be accepted. They were already marked as outsiders and that's where they'd stay.

He inspected each face that leered at him, one by one, without directly staring at them. No one seemed dangerously hostile, which lowered his anxiety a notch, but at the same time he knew there would always be the truculent stares and off-color remarks. Every hour of every day would be a trial, as it was on his last ship, the Indianapolis. With the realization of what was in store, his spirits sank to a new low, settling near the murky rock bottom of his soul.

He pulled himself to his feet and studied his surroundings. Chaos—hoses snaked between piles of machine parts, power tools, oily rags, and scraps of rusted steel. Shirtless men with grease-stained bodies chipped at rust while welders used acetylene torches to mend bulkhead seams. The repeating thunderclap of metal striking metal reverberated belowdecks.

He stepped over a pile of debris to stand next to his seabag. A brass plaque on the bulkhead informed him that this ship was named after Chester H. Pilgrim, a battleship commander who had died in the North Atlantic during the First World War.

Chief Henry Swiftcreek Ogden marched up and scrutinized the four newcomers. His stout body had an imposing posture. Two scars cut across his cheek. Cobweb-like lines etched his iodine-colored face from hairline to Adam's apple, covering everything except his stony eyes. He made a sound, more of a grunt than a word, but it carried a truculent undertone that conveyed an unmistakable disapproval.

Andrew glanced at Mitchell, searching for some kind of protection.

As crewmen rigged the hoist to haul the whaleboat aboard, Mitchell told Ogden, "Chief, issue these new men bunks and assign them to watches. I'll interview them before lunch."

"Aye, aye, sir. You men grab your shit and follow me."

The chief glared at Grady and Andrew. He gestured with his head toward the bow and sauntered to the crew's quarters under the forecastle deck. The men hoisted their gear and followed.

While Andrew balanced his seabag on his shoulder, he sneaked another glimpse at Mitchell. A shy grin lifted the ends of Andrew's mouth. He felt a shimmer of adoration for the man without knowing precisely why. As he turned to follow his shipmates, the grin retreated and, reminding himself of survival rule number one, his body moved with a deliberate swagger.

# Also from DSP Publications

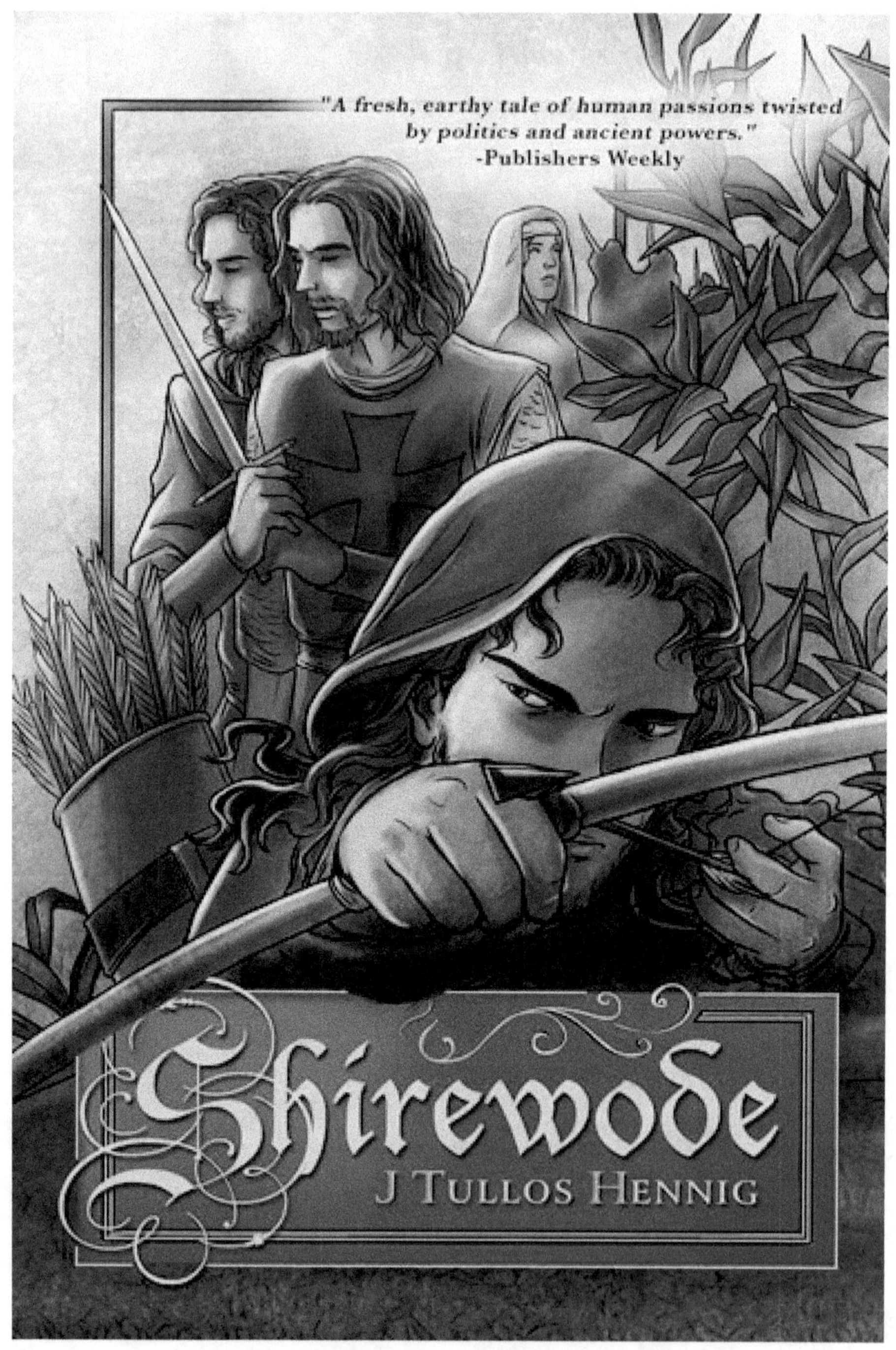


www.dsppublications.com

For more
great fiction
from

# DSP PUBLICATIONS

visit us online.
WWW.DSPPUBLICATIONS.COM